PRAISE FOR
THE TRUE LIES OF REMBRANDT STONE:

"Cast the First Stone is a mind-bender of the first order. Fast paced, strong characters, great twists and Rembrandt Stone is a hero I predict will be grabbing readers around the throat for a long time. This is one to pick up because you won't want to put it down."

~Ted Dekker – New York Times bestselling author

"Cast the First Stone grabs the crime genre by the collar and shows it a thing or two! With time travel, cold cases, and flawed, relatable characters who feel like old friends, this story hooked me from the very first line.

Sleep? Who needs sleep? Give me a True Lies of Rembrandt Stone novel. Masterful writing from three powerhouse storytellers."

-Tosca Lee – New York Times bestselling author

"A thrilling tale from an exciting new voice. The combination of Susan May Warren, James L. Rubart and newcomer David Curtis Warren is seamless. Even better, CAST THE FIRST STONE, utterly shines."

~Rachel Hauck – New York Times Bestselling author

"Holy what?! DO NOT MISS THIS STORY!

David James Warren kills it with this time-travel story that explores regrets and mistakes and the importance of living in the now. I tried explaining to Rembrandt Stone the dangers of messing with the timeline, but would he listen? Of course, not.

This was truly a riveting story that gutted me!

Now. Where the fluff is book 2?"

~Ronie Kendig – author of the bestselling

THE TRUE LIES
OF REMBRANDT STONE

CAST THE FIRST STONE

TriStone Media Group
Minneapolis, MN

Tristone Media Inc.

15100 Mckenzie Blvd

Minnetonka, Minnesota, 55345

Copyright © 2021 by Tristone Media

ISBN: 978-1-954023-00-0

www.RembrandtStone.com

Soli Deo Gloria

CHAPTER 1

It's the regrets that keep me awake.

The broken hearts, the lives ripped apart. The bitter finales.

The sense that, frankly, it's not finished.

I'm not finished, no matter how much I try to lie to myself.

With every crime, a clock starts ticking. A forty-eight hour fuse that ignites, chewing away at the evidence. It begins with the victim and from that moment, time gnaws at every scrap of evidence. Eyewitness memories fade, clues are scattered to the wind by the daily congestion of life.

The colder the trail grows, the lower the likelihood of finding the perpetrators. This accounts for hundreds of thousands of cold cases in dusty file rooms and backup databases around the world.

It also accounts for the fist in my gut every time I have to face the bereaved with a despairing update. And, for too long, it accounted for the indentation in a stool down at the Gold Nugget where Jericho Bloom started pouring the minute I darkened the door.

Days past, but the cases still haunt me, some waking me in the still of night, Eve's sleeping body like an anchor in the darkness, tethering me to the now. Sometimes she too, awakens, and knowing, finds me and urges the ghosts to quiet, tucking them back inside.

They never stay silent for long. The whispers always return.

What if?

What if I could go back to the moment, the beginning of the forty-eight hour window? What if I had been smarter or faster? Maybe everything would be different.

But you can't change the past.

None of this is any consolation to the seven-year-old cherub standing in front of me.

"I'm sorry. Gomer's been missing over a month." I'm using my most stoic, former homicide Inspector voice, despite the pull of those big blue eyes staring at me. "I don't have any leads—"

"But Daddy, you're a detective." My accuser has curly, golden blonde hair and the way she stares at me, hands on her hips, so much belief in her eyes, I am undone. "You know how to find things."

Except for Eve, standing in the door frame, her arms folded over her chest, I would make a thousand promises, swear on my soul to unearth the ratty bear I gave Ashley three years ago. Just a gift shop souvenir, a desperation offering because, in the chaos of the moment I'd forgotten her birthday. Of course, out of all the things I gave her, this stupid bear has to be the one she cherishes.

Eve quirks an eyebrow. Her curly auburn hair is tied up, as tidy as she can make it, but corkscrews fall from behind her ears and for a moment, the swift memory of earlier this morning, the softness of her hair between my fingers, derails me.

"Please, Daddy. I miss him. It's all I want for my birthday— Gomer back."

Of course it is.

Ashley inherited her mother's stubbornness, something that has probably kept her mom and me together, a chronic commitment-phobe, this long. She too raises an eyebrow, the expression of an only child who, more than likely, knows the power she has over me. The tiny scar just above her forehead where she ran into a pole at the park is just fading, but the memory of all that blood can still make me nauseous.

There is nothing I won't do for her, and we all know that.

She's wearing a dress—refuses anything else—and isn't moved by the voices gathering in the back yard.

Answers. We all want them, and yes maybe Eve is right—Ash is too old to need a teddy bear. But I'm her father. "Okay, baby. I'll find Gomer, I promise."

I hear a huff in the corner, and I catch Eve rolling her eyes even as she turns away.

But I see the smirk, the *I-knew-it* grin.

Once a detective, always a detective, perhaps. Something I should probably get around to admitting.

"Thank you, Daddy!" I get a quick hug before Ash heads downstairs.

I'm not even sure where to look for the confounded bear, but I do a cursory walk-through of Ashley's bedroom, stopping at the window to peer down at the street. A vehicle has pulled up to the curb, and I spot Silas O'Roarke getting out of his SUV with his daughter. It parches me a little to know that Eve invited him, but she doesn't burn bridges. And, with Eve, a party isn't a party unless *everyone* is included.

I paste on my game face and head downstairs. I've thrown a sheet over the construction debris in the dining room, but the place hangs heavy with the scent of sawdust and stain.

Eve is waiting for me in the kitchen, slicing a watermelon. Outside, the handful of the younger guests are playing on the swing set I spent all of last weekend, and then some, building. A couple parents—neighbors—are helping themselves to the adult beverages. I step up to my wife, pressing a kiss to the nape of her neck, the memory of her scent still swirling inside me.

"I'm going to chop a finger off if you keep doing that," she says, glancing up at me.

I reach around and grab a piece of the fruit. She points her weapon at me, turning in my arms. Hazel-green eyes, soft curves despite her toned body—the woman is tenacious about her morning runs—and a tolerance for my eccentricities that still astounds me.

I'm not sure how I got this lucky, but a guy with my history shouldn't ask too many questions.

I kiss her, quickly, even as she puts a hand to my chest, pushes me away. "Hey, Silas," she says over my shoulder.

I turn, holding out a hand.

Her former assistant, now armed with his own prestigious title, meets my grip.

"Rembrandt." He gives me a small nod, but no smile.

"Silas." Two could play that game. He's never been fond of me. Told me flat out once that I'm not good enough for Eve. I guess we agree on that.

"Play nice you two." Eve uses the tone that earned her the August Vollmer Forensic Science award, and waves her knife. "Don't make me use this."

"You're scaring me," I say as Silas herds his daughter—Cyra—to the backyard.

"Somebody should." Eve hands me the bowl of watermelon.

Maybe I should be scared, because Eve really can handle herself. The product of being the only daughter of a cop, and surrounded by brothers.

I take the bowl outside, into the heat and sunshine. Overhead, the sky is a brilliant blue, a perfect Memorial Day weekend, the redolence of cut grass and lilacs in the fresh Minnesota breeze.

Not a day for darkness, for memories, the kind that could cut a man to his soul, so I force away the familiar, murky ache and smile for the gaggle of little girls and their parents.

Why remember anyway? I have too much good in my life to let the past steal it.

At least that's what I tell myself.

My neighbor Russell—former lineman for the Vikings, and current attorney—lifts his sweating Stella to me even as he continues his conversation with Gia, from across the street. Gia is dark-haired, petite, curvy and newly single, separated from Alex who moved out in a loud domestic event two weeks ago. Eve and I watched from our porch, her hand on my arm. I wasn't sure if she was holding me back or waiting to push me into the fight.

Frankly, I wasn't sure myself. My instincts are a little off after three years away from the force.

Russell is leaning down, his attention back on Gia and I fear there's more to the conversation than I want to know.

Perhaps my instincts aren't as off as I think.

Silas has helped himself to a beer in the cooler—he's used to Eve's expectations by now—and pops the top with his ring as he comes back to stand by me. "They grow up too fast," he says, referring to Cyra and Ashley and the rest of the first graders. "How's the book coming?"

Small talk, because he's a bright guy, a crime scene investigator and one look at my house suggests an answer.

Apparently, writer's block can't be solved by remodeling the kitchen, building out the back deck or re-tiling the fireplace in our 1930s craftsman.

"It's coming." Silas is the last person I'm about to let dig away at my choices. That critique, I leave to Burke.

"Keeping busy?" I counter. "Lots of crime in Minnetonka these days?"

I mean it as a joke, sorta, but I can almost hear Eve in my ears, *don't start. Some people want the suburban life.*

"Enough," Silas says, his mouth tightening at the corners. We're opposites of the same coin, perhaps. He's a sandy blonde to my dark brown, although his hair is cut short, and yeah, I'm starting to resemble a clichéd version of reclusive author, my hair long and curly behind my ears. Eve can nearly grab it into a ponytail. She doesn't hate it, though—or at least I don't think so, given the way she plays with it when we watch T.V. Silas is about my build, six foot flat-footed, and although I have a couple years on him, I've kept up my workouts. I could still take him in a pickup game.

Or in other games.

Silas's gaze flickers to Cyra and Ash, comparing, maybe, the way it all worked out. I see old stories, old recriminations rising in his pale green eyes.

If he'd had his way, Eve would be living in some modern rambler on an acre lot overlooking a biking trail in some oak-shaded safe suburban neighborhood.

Instead, she landed a vintage fixer upper with character, situated just a few blocks off Lake Calhoun, in the shadow of Minneapolis, on a postage stamp lot.

With me.

I walk over to the cooler to grab a cold beer.

Ash is swinging, her pumps arcing her high into the wind, and I want to tell her to be careful. The words are almost out when a scream—followed by a word the seven-year-olds shouldn't hear—turns me on my heel.

A crash, and I'm at the door, barreling inside.

Eve is standing at the sink, her hands in front of her, deflecting the spray of a broken faucet, the shards of a glass bowl littering the basin. "Rem! You told me you fixed this!"

I move her out of the way—the spray hits me full on, soaking through my T-shirt, my jeans—and I cup my hand over the torrent, even as I try and shunt the flow. "Turn off the water under the sink!"

"What—?"

I grab a towel and shove it over the spray, deflecting it down and hit my knees, digging out the cleaning products that clutter the cupboard before finding the shut off valve.

The spray dies and I sit for a moment in a puddle on our new wood floor. Eve is standing over me, and she's not amused, the water turning her white blouse nearly transparent, her hair dripping. She picks up a towel and presses it into the ends of her hair.

"I'm a writer, not a plumber."

She rolls her eyes, and that hurts just a little, but she offers me her hand. "You're a detective. Figure out why my faucet is busted."

Like daughter, like mother. "The rubber gasket on the seal is leaking." I hear the doorbell and add, "You should go change." I'm thinking of Silas, but I'm not keen on Russell getting a glimpse of the goods either.

She tosses the towel in the sink and I head to the door.

My step hiccups just a second before I open it because I recognize the man through the side lights.

Tall, skin the color of a starless night, bald, and by his stance, still training weekly at Quincy's. He's staring at the door as if he'd like to take it out with his X-ray vision. He's holding a file box almost like a shield.

This will be fun.

I open the door. "Burke."

"Sorry, I'm late."

He's not on the list, but of course Eve would have invited him. He offers me a smile, and I know he's trying. But you don't partner with a guy for nearly twenty years without knowing his tells, when and why he'd flinch, and most importantly, the ability to read the disappointment in his eyes.

Frankly, I've sort of gotten used to it.

"No problem."

He sets the box down on a bench by the door. I recognize the handwriting, the frayed edges of the cardboard, the warped fit of the cover, and can't help but react. "What is that doing here?"

"It showed up at the station with a note for you." Burke lifts a shoulder. "Part of his estate, I guess."

Police Chief John Booker, having the last word. Of course. "I thought the files were destroyed when we scanned them into the database."

Burke glances at the box and for a second, we stand in silence, the memory of John Booker between us. Regrets and what-ifs and the burning is back inside my gut.

Oddly, and maybe for the first time ever, I'm saved by my parents strolling up the walk.

"Rembrandt," my father says, landing on our wide porch. He still carries himself like the farmer-slash-builder he is, and I'm sure we'll later have a dissection of my current projects. Wide-shouldered, his hair now fully gray and thinning, Vincent Stone bears the scars in his countenance of holding us all together—well, at least my mother—during the years of wondering, a decade of grief and anger and questions that held us hostage.

This week is the unfortunate anniversary of the discovery of my brother's remains, twenty-three years ago, and I can see it lurking behind my mother's smile as she arrives. She still walks with a cane, sometimes struggles to form words, the right side of her face sags, always at half-pout.

In this way, it's always with us, Mickey's murder, embedded in our bones. But like good Minnesotans, we don't talk about it, tuck it away along with the anger, the frustration.

But sometimes, there's just nothing to say.

"Mom," I say and give her a hug. Her bones are fragile beneath my touch, and she's lost more weight, her crazy no salt diet stripping the fat from her bones. "You look good," I add, because that's our way.

She pats my cheek, knows that I'm lying. "Where's my favorite granddaughter?" Her words are slushy, but we're all used to that and I understand her perfectly. *Her favorite granddaughter.* It's just a funny thing she says—because we all know Ash is her *only* granddaughter.

"In the backyard. Waiting for you." I wink and it feels like we've put ourselves back together, that we're going to be okay, for one more day.

My dad comes in and I know I should mention the fact that it's his birthday week too. But we long ago stopped celebrating anything—birthdays, Christmas, Thanksgiving. After all, what did we have to be thankful for?

They head into the backyard and it's then that I turn and, on a crazy whim I know I'll pay for, I rip free the packing tape on the box and peek inside one edge of the cover.

Inside, nearly packed to the rim, lay files and files of my old cases. Cold cases. Failures, frustrations, and everything I hated about my job.

The cases that won't let me sleep.

Thank you, John Booker. In his last vengeful act, he gave them to me. Punishment for not being the guy he wanted me to be, maybe.

I pick up the box (the last thing I want is for someone to root through these) and head into my office, a room at the front of the house, away from the chaos of the kitchen.

There's a smell to my office—coffee, old books, the leather from a chair Eve bought right after I left the force—that should inspire me, I'm sure of it. I even have the cover of my first—and currently, *only*, book—on my wall. Success, right?

I'm starting to think that first blockbuster is a fluke, a literary anomaly. I'm sure my agent thinks this too, but his emails to me are full of *how's that new ending going*, and *we have publishers interested*.

Everyone, trying to keep me from wallowing in the dark truth.

I blew it, and big, and there's no going back to the life I had. The career, the legacy that I was *good*, painfully good, at.

What's left is my screen saver swirling against a blackness, hiding an empty page.

I set the box on my desk—the first table Eve and I bought together—careful not to bump the mouse, then I leave. Shut the door.

Because that's where the stories, and the memories, and even the failures should stay. Locked under the cover of darkness.

I turn back to the party, the wounds fresh and pulsing in my gut, now keenly reminded of the brutal truth.

Try as I might, there are no happy endings.

CHAPTER 2

The worst part about the dream is the helplessness. You know what I mean, the way you watch from the outside, your feet cemented, your body encased in a sort of glue, and even the words issuing from your mouth are garbled as you scream for everything to *stop*. Or in the case of this particular re-occuring nightmare—to *run*.

Please, Oh, God, *run*.

Because every single time I'm standing on the corner, screaming, as a young mother, her toddler on her hip, goes into the Daily Grind coffee shop. That's when my heart starts pounding, my breathing thickens, and the sweat coats my body because I *know* her. She's Melinda Jorgenson, and in her identification photo she had blonde hair, was wearing a pair of yoga pants, a T-shirt and tennis shoes. In my dream, she's fresh from her morning walk and meeting her mother—I don't remember what she looks like. Most importantly, she is carrying her two-year-old son.

Blue eyes. Blond curls. He's holding a Beanie Baby, a frog, I think.

The dream is merciful. It never recalls the after photos or Silas's gruesome scene shots. Some things a detective, no matter how much he's seen, just never forgets, and Melinda Jorgenson clutching her towheaded kid in death is one of them.

But in my dream, they're always alive for at least ten agonizing seconds while I stand in the cement, screaming at the top of my lungs.

Run.

The building explodes and although I expect it, I still flinch. Dust and smoke boil out, flames sear the morning air, and only then does the scream break free.

I've learned to shut my horror down before it breaks the veneer of slumber, at least most of the time. But I wake to my whimpers, my heart a fist against my chest, thundering in my ears.

My body is shaking, the sweat coating my chest as I wake now. The room is pitch, just the blood red glow of the numbers on the alarm clock against the ceiling. The whir of the fan is a hum, rhythmic and safe.

I'm not standing on a street corner watching people burn alive.

I loosen my hold on my sheets, kick them off and just breathe.

Seven people died that morning. If I think hard, I can probably remember their names. Memory is cruel that way—it steals the moments you want to save, and leaves behind the rubble.

Eve stirs beside me and rolls over. "Babe, you're sweating." Her eyes open and she raises herself onto her elbow. "Which dream was it? The ice—?"

"The bombing."

She makes a noise of understanding, her hand trailing up to reach my face, hold it.

"It's okay." I weave my fingers through hers. "Go back to sleep."

She drifts back to her side and climbs back under a mountain of covers, dressed in long pajamas, despite the relative summer heat. She's always cold, and when we were first married she would press her iceberg feet to my legs and chill me to the bone. She wears wool socks now—it's simply easier, maybe than to wait for me to come to bed. I miss her toes against my skin.

Tonight, she escaped upstairs shortly after my parents left while I wrestled with the leaky faucet, avoiding the file box in my office.

The after pictures of Melinda Jorgenson and her son have found me, however, so I get up, walk to the bathroom, and shut the door. The light burns the images away and when I scrub some water on my face, it flushes away the memory enough for me to find myself.

I'm awake, edgy, and not a little peeved, so I flick off the light and creep across the room and litter of pillows on the floor. Our dog—no, Eve's dog, a tiny salt-and-pepper rescue mutt named Oliver—lifts his head from one of the mounds, but deems me inconsequential and goes back to sleep.

Apparently, I do this too often for Oliver to get worked up.

But it's the quiet hours that lure me to the muse, to prod at the words that seem to hide when the light of day hits. In truth, I'm a thief, searching for story as I sneak around my house in the middle of the night.

God, please I'm begging you, if you're up there, give me words.

The moon is striping the floor outside Ashley's room, pale fingers beckoning me to linger. So I do, then tiptoe in because my seven-year-old sleeps like me—her covers in a tangled mess. But she possesses the body temperature of her mother, so I straighten them out, pull them up and burrito her inside them. The light through her shuttered blinds turns her hair white, her cute pink mouth puckered up. She's curled around a stand-in for Gomer, some counterfeit friend she pulled from her wealth of stuffed animals shoved into the closet and spilling out into her room.

She is spoiled, I know it and I don't care. I'm not unaware of how lucky I am that she is alive, healthy, happy and mine. And Eve along with her.

It's these little moments that can break me, and I blow out a breath and lean down, press a kiss to that downy cheek.

Then I creep down to my study.

It's just how I left it, the file box on the desk, the computer icon swirling. I shut the door. Flick on my desk lamp.

Light puddles against the file box and for a long second, I debate.

But I know what's in there without looking, thanks, so I set it on the floor and with a shove of my bare foot push it away, next to the leather chair that is supposed to inspire me with deep thoughts.

Instead I sit down on the padded office chair Eve got me for Christmas and, with a breath, wiggle the mouse.

It's still there, still waiting for me to end the sentence, the cursor blinking as if asking where I've been.

I'm mid-scene, my hero—a police Inspector (what else would I write about?) is dissecting the remains found at the scene of a bombing with the local crime scene investigator.

Okay, I admit it, I don't have a lot of imagination, and yes, I pulled from what I know. Although I'm a lot less paunchy than my protagonist, and Eve probably wouldn't approve of my portrayal of her character. More cleavage, a little more sass, although that's not a complaint on the prototype.

Fiction, I'm discovering, is harder than writing true crime. For one, in true crime, there's an ending, although not usually a happy one.

Apparently, a happy ending is some kind of requisite in fiction, an argument my agent and I keep circling.

I start at the top and begin to read.

Butcher found Gabby leaning over her microscope, her eye pressed to the lens, a dozen micro-slides lined up beside her.

"Any luck?"

"You'd better have coffee when you slink in this late," she said, not looking up.

"Why aren't you at home?" He didn't mean his tone. It just wasn't always easy to keep his thoughts straight around Gabby. She wore her dark hair back in a ponytail, no makeup. Pretty despite her shapeless medical garb.

"I found something." She got up and went over to a table of twisted black wiring, plastic, and other bomb debris, all labeled. "The bomb was on a timer. I found the remnants of an alarm clock. It's a simple design, but effective."

Butcher took it apart. "He planted it, then walked away to watch."

"Mmmhmm."

The cursor blinks. Now what?

I know what *did* happen next. Next, his partner comes in and drags him away to shoot darts down at the Gold Nugget, missing a perfect opportunity to discuss with *ahem,* Gabby, not just the case but maybe add a little heat to the spark between them.

Geez, I was stupid back then.

"Rem?"

Although the voice is soft, I still jump, and then feel a little silly sitting here in my pajama bottoms, bare-chested, staring at my screen.

Eve shuffles in and sits down in my not-so-inspirational chair. Her auburn hair is down, curly, worry in her pretty hazel-green eyes. "The dream, again?"

I shrug.

"You have to let it go."

"I did. I have. It's just—" And then my eyes betray me because they fall on the file box. And the last—*the very last*—person I should tip off about Booker's final gift to me is my wife. She's like a bird dog when she scents a mystery and the fact that former Inspector John Booker would save—and send me—these files is like throwing a pheasant in front of a Labrador retriever.

Poor woman simply can't help but pounce.

In a second, she has the top off and has pulled out the first couple files. "These are—wow."

"I know," I say, but I'm not going to touch them. Especially if I want to get any sleep in the near future.

"There are at least thirty cases in here."

A tiny swell of relief hits me. So, Booker didn't include *all* of my cold cases. "Which ones?" Okay, I confess, I'm just a little intrigued.

She has them piled on her lap, and is sorting through them, by dates. "There's that case about the girl who was found in the alley outside Sunny's."

Right. I remembered her. A working girl, about nineteen, she'd died early in the morning, the last John's payment still in her pocket.

"And the one about that waitress—strangled in a parking lot near Lulu's diner."

"Those are all in my early years of being an Inspector." I slide down to the floor and notice her eyes darken as she picks up one of the thickest files. "What?"

"Nothing."

Aw, c'mon. I wasn't a detective for nothing. "Tell me."

"It's the coffee shops bombing file." She makes a face.

I take a breath. Yeah, if John had collected my early career top hits then he would have surely included the coffee shop bombings. Plural. Three bombings, all within 48 hours of each other in the Minneapolis area. Twenty lives in total. Then they simply stopped. And are still unsolved, Melinda Jorgenson and her son's murderer still at large.

No wonder I can't sleep.

I reach for the file, but Eve pulls it away. "No. It's no good sifting through it again. We went over every stitch of evidence. I spent hours and hours and hours…"

"I know," I say. "I remember. You were obsessive, too."

She sighs. "It was my first big case. My first real opportunity to show my dad…" And now she swallows, looks away and I want to get my hands around John Booker's dead throat and squeeze. Because it wasn't long after this that Eve's father was killed by a drive-by shooter linked to one of his cases. And with him, her kid brother, Ash.

Bittersweet memories for all of us because it was her grief and desire for justice that drove her into my arms the first time.

She closes the file. Presses a hand on it.

Like always, I have to fix it. "I've always told you that was the moment I fell for you. I'll never forget walking onto the scene and seeing you standing there. I'd heard about this whiz crime scene investigator, and there you were—"

"And I'd been warned by everyone—including my dad—to stay far away from the infamous lady-killer Rembrandt Stone."

"There were no ladies slain on my watch." But I've made her smile.

"Oh, you thought you were all that, though, Rem. You came striding into the crime scene, the cracker-jack detective, carrying a cup of coffee, as if you were there to watch us work, then you spilled it all over me, and I dropped my camera."

"*You* knocked the coffee out of my hands. I wasn't fast enough to grab the camera."

"You were standing right behind me. Invading my personal space."

"Checking you out, actually."

"I knew it." She's really grinning now.

"You were so beautiful, I couldn't think straight. I nearly said it right then, just blurted it out. At least I got your attention, though."

"Yeah, which you conveniently used to wheedle me into a first date."

"*Charm* you. And you turned me down. Even though I know you were in love with me, too."

She's full-out laughing now, and the sound pours light into my darkness.

"Lie to yourself all you want, Rembrandt Stone. But I'll never forget the look on your face when you busted my camera. Half angry, half embarrassed. You were trying to figure out what to do, and I kept thinking, here I was, smitten with you because you were this hot shot, New York Times bestselling author, and suddenly all I saw was this flustered guy. It made me…I don't know, maybe I fell in love with you that moment."

"You didn't act like it. You were so angry—"

"My camera was broken. Besides, I could hardly let on that I liked you. I had a reputation for not dating anyone I worked with. In fact, if you hadn't spilled coffee on me, I probably wouldn't have spoken to you again, at least not outside the job."

"Why not?"

"Because you're hard to get to know—*really* know. But you showed me a glimpse of yourself, and followed it up with an apology coffee, all humble and sweet and what could I do? I hate playing games, and you cut right to the chase. I suddenly discovered the guy behind his reputation."

"So, you're saying you're glad I ruined your camera."

"It was a Canon EOS-3, worth about five thousand dollars, so, uh no—"

"I'm kidding. But it did give me a reason to talk to you again. I'm not sure I would have had the guts, otherwise."

"Why?"

"Because you were Danny Mulligan's daughter. And there were non-negotiable rules to keep."

"You like breaking the rules." She runs her fingers over the veins in the top of my hand.

"Yeah, I do," I say, my breath catching. "Especially with you."

Silence, and the memories are thick between us. "We had a lot of fun back then." Her voice is soft.

"If you call spending too many hours with crime scene evidence, fun."

"I do." She takes her hand away to trace the sticker on the top of the file. She's blinking. "I *did*."

I look away. Because our glory days as Eve and Rembrandt, CSI and hot shot detective are over.

She gathers up the folders, and I notice she's putting them—at least the first few—in order. Another thing she can't help. "Eve—"

"It's okay, Rem. I understand."

It's a canned, practice response. *It's okay, Rem. I understand.*

She wants to, I know it. She understands loss, and frustration and even helplessness, but she wasn't there the day when my future looked me in the eye, and I surrendered.

Wasn't there for the fight between Booker and me. Didn't hear the words.

I can't go back.

But I pretend her words help, nod and help her stack the files. That's what marriage is about, sometimes, agreeing that the lies are truth.

Leaning up to put the files away, Eve hesitates and then, cradling the stack in one arm, grabs something from inside the box. "Look at this."

She hands me a watch.

It's a vintage watch, very old, the kind that needs winding and even as I take it, I glimpse a visage of John sitting at his desk, playing with the dial. I lay it out in my hand. It's cool and heavy and the memory takes root. Chief Booker wore this every day that I knew him. The watch face is an old friend, see-through to the gears inside, with hatches that mark the time, bigger at the quarter hour. Almost as wide as my thumb, the band is leather, fraying at the edges, the clasp a little bent.

The tiny gears sit unmoving, hands stuck at 3:27 as I spin the dial. It moves, but nothing turns. Of course it's broken. Turning it over, I read an inscription on the backside. *Be Stalwart.* The etching is written in script, and it's faded, the edges smooth, aged.

"John gave you his watch." It's not a question, but more of a breath from Eve, a moment of wonder.

"No. It probably fell in there." I start to hand it to her, but she shoves it back to me. "He gave you his watch, Rem. When did you ever know John Booker to do anything by accident?"

She's right, as usual, but especially with John, the most serious, darkly purposeful man I've ever met. He never did anything without forethought.

He was my mentor, the man I wanted to be my father, and the person who believed in me when I didn't.

"It's his way of forgiving you," she says, and I look up at her. Frown.

I didn't realize she saw it that way, and it stops me, a little pinch in my gut. I'm about to retort that I wasn't the one who needed forgiveness, but it's late, and I don't want a fight.

And deep down inside, I fear she's right.

She puts the files in the box as I rub my thumb over the inscription. Stalwart. An old word that means loyal. Reliable. Hardworking.

Everything I thought I was. Or wanted to be.

Eve has terrifying mind-reading powers because she takes the watch from my hand and puts it on the desk. "He gave it to the right person."

I look away, but she touches my face. "I love you, Rem."

Then she flicks off the light and leads me back up the stairs.

And in the silk of the night, she does her best to convince the past to set me free.

Chapter 3

I work from home. This is not the same as being a stay-at-home dad, although it can feel the same sometimes when I'm the only one around to bring Ashley's forgotten lunch to school or show up in the carpool line to drive her home. I'll even take her to the park, but I bring my iPad with me and spend some time catching up on my Star-Trib reading, (and maybe a little solitaire).

The mothers talk about me, sitting across the sandy pit at a picnic table, waving occasionally. I can't hear them, but I know their words.

Poor man, doesn't he have a job?

I do. I will. I refuse to be sucked into the temptation to drop into their laps one of my many garage-storage copies of *The Last Year*.

However, I admit to keeping a box in the trunk of my car. Just, in case.

They invite me over sometimes, and I'm nice, because, like I said, Eve doesn't burn bridges.

I do. With a flourish, and plenty of gasoline and explosives.

Eve's way might be better.

I'm not on playground—or even school drop off—duty today. Eve and Ashley are gone by the time I finish my run, 3.2 miles around Lake Calhoun. I brace my hands against the shower tile, letting the cool water sluice between my shoulder blades, trying to work it out.

He gave you his watch, Rem. When did you ever know John Booker to do anything by accident?

Eve's right, I know it in my bones, and the question is a burr under my skin. Forgiveness? Maybe. But like I said, I'm not the one who needed forgiving.

So, something else then. While John had a little bit of cowboy in him, the kind of guy who, in earlier days might have shot first and asked questions later, he wasn't vindictive.

Just, immovable.

One might say, *stalwart.*

I wish there was someone to ask—Burke, maybe, but he left shortly after we cut the cake yesterday, and it's not like he's going to disagree with Eve. He probably considers himself on that list of people I need to apologize to, except he knows me, so he's not holding his breath.

We've managed to find a tenable peace, dodging the what-ifs in our weekly workouts and occasional go-arounds in the ring. We're a fair match, but I see the satisfaction in his eye when he lands the occasionally bell-ringing shot. I look up at him from the mat and he's fighting a smile.

Enjoy it, pal, because that's all the apology you're ever going to get.

The windows are open, the day bright and cheery as I go downstairs, neatly avoiding the office, for now, and head into the kitchen.

Eve has left me coffee and I fill my cup, grab a piece of cold bacon, soggy on a paper towel near the stove and am mentally checking off my to-do list on the re-staining of the baseboard in the dining room when my gaze lands on a scrap of paper on the counter.

A torn out yellow page. I walk over and see it's the watch repair listings. Across the top, Eve has scribbled one word in a black sharpie. *Go.*

Maybe I'll never know why John left me his watch, but something about the word etched in the back, along with Eve's nudge has me latching onto the idea that this is my chance to find out, maybe lance the festering.

Not ask for forgiveness, let's make that clear. But just to seal up the dark ache inside.

Besides, I can almost hear her. *You're an Inspector, Rem. Figure it out.*

Was. *Was* an Inspector.

I pull up a Google map of the first place. It's just a couple miles away in Uptown, so how long can it take?

Folding the listing, I shove the paper into my jeans pocket, stop by the office to grab the watch off the desk and head outside.

I get my passion for vintage German automotive technology from my dad. He had a private love affair with a 1962 VW Bug that we spent years in our garage restoring, but I have more elegant tastes.

I'm a sucker for the 911 Porsches, especially the 993 GT2 line. Turbos, they're called, and in 1985 Porsche took the 911 Turbo, twin-turbo, flat-six engine and combined it with a wide-body, rear-drive chassis to create a beautiful machine. Side canards and a massive rear wing with air scoops, it was also upgraded under the hood, it got a bump to 429 hp—which meant zero to sixty in 3.9

seconds, top speed 187 mph. Porsche only made fifty-seven of these beauties, the last of the air-cooled engines and fate smiled down on me the day a guy who called himself Biggie North got picked up on 35W doing a Hasselhoff, as if the three-lane freeway might be the Autobahn. Poor girl was coughing her way down the highway, finally sputtered out and shut down right there in the middle lane. Highway patrol snagged Biggie on a dozen other warrants and my dream girl got hauled off to impound.

A month later, she auctioned off at exactly the spare change in my recently flush savings account.

I spent the next year under the hood, replaced the timing belt, rebuilt the carburetor, got her purring, then turned to the interior where I ripped out the red carpet, replaced it with utilitarian black, shined up the leather seats and since then she's been a guy's best friend.

Always hot, always ready to go. I know I sound about twenty-six, but a guy needs a way to remember who he was.

Eve hates the car. Makes me drive the Ford Escape when I take Ashley to school, even though Ash would choose the Porsche every time.

I slide in, open the T-roof and turn on KQ92 as I pull out.

I tap out Haddaway's, "What is Love," on the steering wheel as I cruise around the lake. There are still a few runners out as the sun climbs the sky, the lake rippling under the brush of the wind. I like the energy of Uptown, the specialty delis, the mix of vintage theaters and shiny new gyms and eclectic whole food cafés. There's something for everybody, and it never bores.

I'd die a slow death in the suburbs, and so would Eve. She loves heading up her own gritty crime scene investigation department downtown, and she might not admit it, but in her own way, she's picked up where her dad left off.

I win a spot with a still flush meter across the street from American Vintage Watch Repair, listed on a tiny door wedged between a Mediterranean Grill and a Deluxe Smokes, e-cigarettes. Following a dim hallway, I discover an office that looks more like my grandfather's old workshop, wooden bench, dim lighting and a thousand crazy screws, washers and tools included.

A giant magnifying glass is mounted to the surface, and at the top, what looks like surgical instruments are fitted into a tray, ready to be plucked for use. Solder equipment, canisters of oils and grease, and over a dozen watches, all antique, hang on a dowel under a hanging fluorescent lamp.

A man sits at the desk, a monocle wedged into his eye, leaning over to examine the finite gears on a pocket watch.

I clear my throat as I stand at the door.

He ignores me.

"I'm wondering—"

He holds up his free hand, cutting off my words, and I watch in silence as he reaches out and grabs, clearly from practice, a pair of tweezers.

I hold my breath as he reaches in and plucks out the offending gear.

Then he sets the gear and the monocle on the desk. He's Asian, dark-skinned, and looks at me as if I've annoyed him.

"You fix watches?"

He stares at me.

I know I sound like a moron, so I pull Booker's watch from my pocket and simply hand it over.

He still says nothing, but takes my watch, turns it over, then back and frowns.

"I can't fix this." He shoves the watch back at me.

"What do you mean? You barely even looked at it." I find myself rubbing my thumb over the inscription.

"I can't fix." He shoos me away with a flick of his hand. Reaches for his monocle.

I'm not quite dismissed, thanks, pal. "Why not?"

"It's not my specialty. Besides, it's not broken."

"What do you mean it's not broken? You can't wind it, see?" I give him a little demonstration, but he shakes his head.

"Okay, fine. Do you know anyone who *can* fix it?"

He puts down his monocle. Purses his lips and reaches for a business card. He writes something on the back and hands it to me.

I turn it over.

It's an address in Stillwater, a tiny town an hour south from here. I know because Eve and I spent our honeymoon there, nearly eight years ago, camped out at a bed and breakfast that overlooked the river.

She was three months pregnant, still nauseated with morning sickness, and even the smell of the gourmet blueberry pancakes sent her running to the bathroom. Not a great start to our life together, and the next six months weren't much better, with her bed rest and a couple of miscarriage scares. We spent the weekend watching old movies on a tiny television set, me running out for special order ice cream.

I'd love to have another go at the whole thing, starting with the fact that it took me nearly a decade to propose. What was I so afraid of?

I glance at the front of the card, mumble a thanks and head back to the street. I climb into the Porsche and sit there for a minute, debating.

I should go home and work on my manuscript.

A slightly better option would be to finish staining the baseboard in the dining room.

Or, I could strike the jackpot and get a call from one of the moms at Ashley's school, and get invited for a play date.

As if my mood has conjured it, my cell rings and I look at caller I.D.. I scowl. My agent. Great. But I've been avoiding him way too long, so, "Frank. How are you?"

Frank Rydlebower hasn't had a publishing triumph in nearly a decade. I know he keeps me around because of the lure of my former success, *The Last Year*, settling in the top ten of *The New York Times* over twenty years ago. He still thinks he can shine me up and sell me to the highest bidder.

We've gotten a few bites, my history at the Minneapolis Police Department still a decent calling card. But apparently, publishers want a *finished* book.

Of all the gall.

"Rembrandt. How's the writing going?"

A convertible eases past me down Lake Street, pumping out Taylor Swift's "Shake it off."

"Making progress." I can lie like a criminal when I need to.

"Good." He hesitates, and suddenly I have the urge to lean my head against the steering wheel and sigh.

"What?"

"I clear my list every year, Rem, and it's been three since you signed with me…"

Aw, shoot. "I'll have something to you by the end of the week," I say, praying this time it's not a lie.

Silence. Then, "Okay, good. You've got another bestseller in you, I know it. Looking forward to reading it."

Yeah, me too. I hang up, knowing I gotta head home. I've got an empty page waiting for me. It can wait a little longer.

I pull out and point the Porsche to the highway, heading south.

It's a gorgeous day, made even more so by the free and easy vibe of the highway, and I crank up my radio. Sure, I grew up in the late 80s, but my music tastes were cut from a staticky Panasonic radio propped up in my dad's garage, pumping out classics.

I queue up my play list. I might have a vintage car, but the sound system is top of the line. The Eagles are singing "Hotel California" as I head south.

For the next hour, I'm free, and cruising, twenty-six and leaving it all behind. I barely look at the map, motoring into Stillwater from memory. I pull into a coffee shop and get out, finding my bearings.

The address is a couple blocks away, so I decide to walk. Never hurts to get the lay of the land.

It's a house. An old white-stucco Tudor with a decaying brick chimney climbing up the front, a quaint rounded top door, with dark stain. I guess I notice those things now—the color of stain, the hosta around the walk, the vintage Japanese maple in the front yard. I'm going to blame my improved home decorating eye on Eve and her laundry list of house upgrades.

I check the address against the metal numbers on the lintel, notice the bars on the tiny square window, and the outer door, then press the bell. A Gothic chime bullies the place and I don't hear the footsteps.

The door opens, and I'm sized up by an elderly gentlemen, so thin his bones protrude from a lined, saggy face. Fraying white hair, gnarled hands, but his eyes bore through me as if, once up on a time, he was somebody that understood what trouble looked like.

Or maybe that's just the bars on the door telling his story.

"Yes?"

I can't tell if he's annoyed or intrigued, so I offer my name, adding, "I was sent here by the Vintage Watch shop guy in Uptown."

He frowns.

"I was hoping…" I pull out the watch.

He stretches out a hand, through the bars, and I hesitate only a moment before dropping it into his grip.

He comes alive as he runs his thumb over the inscription, not unlike I've found myself doing. He fiddles with the dial, then with a quickness that startles me, shuts the door.

What—?

"Hey!" I grab the bars, knock on the door, but it's locked. I lay on the doorbell. "Give me my watch back!"

I'm debating circling around the back when the door pops open and Grandpa is back, holding my watch, a stethoscope hanging from his ears.

Seriously?

He's listening to the watch as if it might have a heartbeat. I stand there awkwardly, waiting for the prognosis.

This is stupid.

But when he hands the watch back to me, I'm oddly hopeful.

Until, "There's nothing wrong with the watch."

Here we go again. "What are you talking about? It doesn't work, see?" I do a demonstration for him, winding the dial, holding it up so he can see the dead-in-their-tracks hands. "Nothing moves."

Grandpa has removed his stethoscope, draping it around his neck. He looks at me with a sort of shake of his head. "The watch is working exactly as it is intended. Didn't anyone show you how to use it?"

I blink at the old man. "No. Actually, I sort of inherited it."

One untrimmed eyebrow goes up. "Certainly you've seen it used."

This rocks me back. "Of course. It was…well, my boss had it, and he gave it to me when he died. But he wore it for years."

This has elicited a response, something of understanding because Grandpa is nodding. "I see."

"But I don't!"

"Just use it like you saw him use it, and it will do its job."

"It doesn't work! It's job is to tell the freakin' time!"

"You're wrong. It's working exactly how it's intended." And with that Grandpa closes the door.

Leaving me to stand on the steps in hot sun.

And now I want to hit something, so maybe it's time for the gym. Because Eve's right. I'm a detective and I want answers.

CHAPTER 4

Quincy's Boxing Gym is located in north Minneapolis in an old warehouse, with a rolling garage door for the entrance. It's hip, with exposed piping, metal beams and tiny boxed warehouse windows that give it a vintage feel. With two sparring rings, ten hanging bags, a free weight room, pull-up and dip bars and plenty of graffiti, the place smells of cement, sweat, and raw, hard work.

The Who is playing at ear piercing volumes as I walk in.

I've been coming here for twenty years, and frankly, it's not for the atmosphere, or the music.

It's because Burke shows up every day at exactly 4:12 p.m., after his day shift ends and once upon a time, it was the one place where we could work off the day.

Now, like I said, I want answers.

It's early so I change, do a few sets with the jump rope, popping a sweat.

I drop for a set of polymeric push ups, flip over and add in some sit ups, then end with a few squat thrusts.

I'm sweating, my body buzzing and I'm ready to hit something.

I tape up and work the speed bag. The Doors sing about lighting my fire, and I'm breathing hard when I see Burke stroll in.

He glances at me, nods, and heads to the locker room.

I finish my speed bag sprint and do some shadowboxing. Then I glove up and I'm at the heavy bag when he emerges.

He steps up to the bag, just to tame it.

I imagine the bag is John Booker and land my fist in the center. I've been at this enough to know how to keep my balance, but I'm still a little unfocused, maybe, so I dig down. I lean in and feel the sharp smack of my fist against the bag, a snapping punch, not a push.

I'm not trying to take myself out, just work off those words. Because what can a watch do if it doesn't tell time?

The bag swings hard, back at me, and I keep my feet light, following it. I don't wait to throw the next punch, because that's for beginners, but dive back in.

I feel Burke at my side before I see him. He catches the bag. "My turn."

I'm breathing harder than I thought and sweat saturates my shirt. Burke works off my mitts, tosses them aside and gloves up.

"What I don't get is why Booker gave me the files. And his watch—did you know about that?"

I don't need a preamble with Burke. He nods and says, "I wondered what this was about."

"Why couldn't he just leave it?"

Burke lifts a shoulder, throws a punch. I'm aware that he hasn't warmed up, but his hit stuns the entire bag, a massive force, and I'm sorta glad we're not sparring.

I'm clearly out of shape and that makes me even more perturbed.

"I'm surprised you're surprised," Burke says, dancing with the bag. "Clearly, he thinks you have unfinished business."

"Half those files are yours."

"I'm still around." He slams his massive paw into the bag, a thud, a through-shot that could break ribs. "Where are you?"

I'm waiting for the uppercut, *how's the book going*, but Burke has mercy and gives it to me square, "You should have never left. Booker—"

"John Booker made me leave."

"Your fear made you leave."

Oh. I've changed my mind. I want back in the ring.

Burke never raises his voice. Ever. It's freaky, but he actually gets quieter and that's when you have to worry. Now, he's just about whispering and frankly, if I had sense, my blood would run cold.

"And your pride kept you from coming back."

I knew he was angry, but maybe I should stand back.

"A cop died that day." I put my hand on the bag, push it back to him. "I had a four-year-old daughter."

"Don't give me that, Rem. You haven't been afraid a day in your life. Then suddenly, you turn in your badge, and it's over?"

Yeah, well, maybe. But that day, three years ago when I saw Jimmy Williams shot in the head, I was afraid in a way I had never considered.

It could have been me, easily, my blood spilled in the middle of Franklin Avenue.

Burke grabs the bag, coming in close for body shots. I wonder if he wishes it was me.

We've had a few go-rounds, Burke and I. That's what happens when you're partners for twenty years. Most of them happened in the early, hot-head, daring rookie days.

A few, later. More consequential. The kind of fights that actually hurt. But mostly we took it to the ring, left a few bruises but stayed friends.

Now, I see that maybe he pulled his punches back then.

"You left because you couldn't stand not being in charge. Booker told you to step back, take leave, but—"

"A cop got killed on my watch. My investigation, my collar. My responsibility."

Burke catches the bag. "Our investigation. Our responsibility."

I say nothing. The place has filled up, a few more familiar faces and I cut my voice as low as Burke's. "I couldn't sit out for three months while IA investigated a clean shooting. The shooter's partner was still out there, and I wasn't going to—"

"Trust me? Because I had your back, Rem. And you should have remembered that before you threw away a twenty-year partnership to write a damn *book*!"

I'm just staring at him because he's *shouting*. Every head swivels our direction.

We're breathing hard, and for a second, I glimpse the past in his eyes. Army brat, son of an angry father. Burke never had anybody but me to call family.

That winds me down, makes me catch my breath. "Of course I trust you."

"Not enough." Burke pushes off the bag and starts tugging at the gloves, one clamped between his legs. "Not like I trusted you."

I feel that hit. I don't help him with his gloves and he doesn't look at me.

He finally works them off, throws them in the bin. Turns. He's found himself again, his voice back to its even keel. "Listen. Those cold cases haunt me as much as they do you. Come back, and let's solve them together."

His eyes are nearly black as they bore into me. Then he turns and heads over to the sparring ring to watch a couple rookies pummel each other.

I take my shower cold, towel off and head home, still wired.

Eve is in the kitchen, plating some fried chicken she picked up at a fast-food joint. She glances over her shoulder, frowns. "You went to work out?"

I nod, and don't mention that I actually spent the day chasing an impulse. "With Burke."

She sucks in a breath, nods. "Well, he's got a good reason to be at the gym today."

I'm not sure to what she's referring except the reason buzzing in my head, and I don't want to talk about it so I head upstairs to drop my gear.

Ashley is playing in her room with her birthday loot from her grandparents, a horse set reminiscent of all the promises I made her to buy her a pony. Someday. I sit down on her floor, in the middle of the pink carpet. "Hey baby, how was your day?"

She gallops a horse up my leg. "Good. But I miss Gomer. Have you found him yet?"

Perfect. "Not yet."

"But you will, Daddy." She smiles at me, her blue eyes bright and shiny.

"Yeah, I will." I kiss her cheek and pry myself off the floor. I'm doing a cursory search of the laundry room, just in case, when Eve calls us downstairs.

She's crafty, that Eve. She's dished up the entire meal—chicken, mashed potatoes, gravy, green beans—as if it might be homemade, and set it on the table. It's important to her to eat like her family did, all six of them at 6 p.m. sharp. Her mother is old school—vegetables, bread, starches, pot roast—it can make Eve a little crazy to try and keep up.

She does well enough for my tastes. I don't remember a home cooked meal beyond the age of twelve.

We sit and Eve makes us pray—it's the Lutheran in her—and we dive in.

She's silent, lost in her thoughts as she flattens her mashed potatoes.

"What?" Instincts.

She glances at Ashley, gnawing on her chicken leg. "It's nothing."

Oh. It's that kind of case.

I turn to Ashley, our talker. She can fill all the gaps between us and she tells me a story about her day that involves something on the playground I probably should be paying attention to, but my gaze is on Eve. And the way she just keeps pounding those mashed potatoes.

Her deep sighs.

The catch of her lower lip between her teeth when she thinks I'm not looking.

Every once in a while, she looks up and feigns a smile.

Something terrible happened.

"Can I be excused?" Little Miss Manners asks and I nearly shoo her away.

Eve has reason to look worried the moment Ashley leaves.

"What is it, babe?"

"I don't want to talk about it."

"Eve—"

"No, it's…" She sighs again and shakes her head. "It's not good timing."

I frown.

"Another teenager was gunned down today, in the Phillips neighborhood."

Oh no. When she meets my eyes, I see compassion. Okay, so the timing sucks and the Somali brotherhood was getting bolder by the day. "How old?"

"Fourteen."

I bite back a swear word because Eve has rules, but yeah, there's a darkness that stirs inside me when a kid gets killed.

She runs her hands down her face. "That's the third girl in three weeks."

I knew that, but hearing it from Eve, the fatigue in her voice, sets a fire deep inside.

Come back, and let's solve them together.

"Listen, Batman, you're off watch. I can handle it." Eve says as she gets up. "I'm going for a run. Make sure Ash doesn't watch any television. I don't want her seeing the news."

I carry my plate to the sink, run water. Dots bead up around the temporary patch I made in the seal around the faucet.

Ashley is sprawled on the sofa, playing some pony video game so I head into my office and sit down at the computer. What kind of idiot promises his agent he'll have something decent in five days?

I pull out the watch, still in my jeans and set it on the desk, then open the screen, and stare at the words.

Nothing.

Eve's footfalls land on the stairs and I hear the front door opening.

"Be careful!" I say, but it closes before I finish. It's daylight, the sun up for at least another hour. And, if I know Eve, she has her phone, her pepper spray and like I said, she grew up with brothers. She knows how to handle herself.

Still, I watch her through my window, her lithe body running down the sidewalk until she disappears from view. Turning back to the computer, my gaze falls on the file box, the lid askew.

Even if I can't go back and solve the cases, maybe they can give me writing inspiration. Yeah, I know, but desperate men reach for desperate options.

Mine includes opening up the bottom drawer of my desk and pulling out the mostly full bottle of Macallan twenty-one-year-old fine oak single malt whiskey.

Don't judge me. The bottle's been here for three years, and it's only four fingers down. I empty another finger into a high ball and shoot it down.

Not a hint of muse stirs inside me so I go over to the file box, paw through the files and find the first one. The coffee shop bombings.

Bring the file back over to my desk. Open it. There, on the front page is my typed summary of the first bombing.

7:06 a.m., Monday morning, at a Daily Grind. Seven lives lost. The store was located just off Franklin Avenue, over the highway from the Phillips neighborhood of Minneapolis.

The first case John mentored me on. I'd forgotten that, how he showed up on the scene and assigned the case directly to me, a young Inspector.

The memory makes me reach over and pick up the watch. I put it on, adjusting the band to fit, and it's oddly warm, as if he just took it off. The fit is right, though, settling in to the groove between my hand and my wrist bone.

Too bad it doesn't work. Almost on impulse, I reach over and twist the dial, like I'd seen John do countless times.

It ticks. Just a heartbeat, soft, as if coming to life. I press it to my ear.

Another tick.

I stare at it, and the second hand moves.

Tick.

Weirdly, the other hands begin to spin. As if possessed of their own power, they turn, counterclockwise, winding backwards in time.

The hour hand settles on seven.

The minute hand lodges just beyond the five.

7:06.

In the distance, an engine roars. I look up, searching for the sound as it grows, sweeps over the room. It's darkening as if a storm cloud has moved in, and as if in evidence, thunder rolls.

I get up and move toward the door. "Ashley!"

I'm not sure what I trip on, but the floor rushes up at me. Something beyond me shatters. Instinctively, I want to duck, but I don't know where the sound issues from. "Ashley—!"

Then it all vanishes. The sound, the darkness, the engine—a hiccup of utter silence, of white, as if I've blinked, except my eyes are open.

I'm standing in a cafe. No, a coffee shop—the deep, earthy scent of freshly ground beans, the churning sound of the grinder, and conversation rising all around me.

I can't place it, but in my bones I know this place. It's an eclectic shop, with a tin ceiling, vintage couches, a brick wall with a graffiti menu, and giant hanging chandeliers.

Eve buys her coffee here. I know this in my gut, and the name of the place is starting to form in my disbelieving brain. *The Cuppa...*

"Sheesh, Rem. Give the ladies a break."

I spin at the voice. Too fast, because the coffee I now realize I'm holding in my hands slams right into—

Oh God, what is happening? Because I've just doused Andrew Burke with some version of a latte, given the color soiling his shirt.

"You've got to be kidding me!" Burke says and I can't get my eyes off him because he has *hair*. And he's slimmer, by about twenty pounds, wiry, and wearing a hint of a soul patch, a dusting of black fuzz.

I mocked it until he shaved it off.

Now it's like a tether, reeling me in.

I scrape up words, anything that might sound coherent when the radio at his belt crackles and a voice scratches through the line.

I don't catch it all, but one code sears into my brain.

10-80.

Explosion.

Just off Franklin.

It's only when Burke grabs my jacket—I'm wearing a freakin' *suit*—and pulls me toward the door that the recognition locks in.

I'm in 1997, and somehow my nightmares have found me.

Chapter 5

Eve Mulligan did not want to live in a war zone one more minute. The chaos of remodeling—the current casualty being the plumbing—just might drive her to murder.

Or at least bodily harm, directed at her younger brother.

"Sams! Turn the flippin' water back on!"

Eve fumbled for the towel, her hand snaking outside the flimsy curtain of her claw-foot tub, suds running into her eyes. She found the towel, grabbed it and shoved it into her face, cleaning out the soap, then turned to fiddle with the faucets. Yes, full on, but not a drip of water from the overhead spigot. "Samson Mulligan, *turn on my water!*"

She nearly fell out of the tub, grabbed her robe and tied her hair up before flinging the door open. Sunlight streamed through the stained-glass transom, casting light down into the upstairs bedroom of her story-and-a-half bungalow. The sound of a saw rumbled up from the kitchen. The dust and the odor of plumber's glue, not to mention freshly stained wood, could turn her woozy.

Her feet ground into the sawdust despite her recent sweep of the stairs, and she barreled down, one hand holding her towel and barged into the kitchen to find—oh no. *Not* her brother Samson bent over his workbench but an unknown plumber, crack and all, leaning over a piece of plastic piping.

A stranger.

In her house.

At 6-freaking-o'clock in the morning.

Her father would have a coronary. And right about now, he might agree with her decision to get a conceal and carry. After all, just because she worked CSI didn't mean she wasn't a *cop*.

The plumber stood up, eyes wide as he took her in—fluffy bathrobe, her hair dripping water down her neck. And not a hot plumber, either, although that might not have changed her indignation. This guy looked about fifty and nursed a beer paunch.

"What are you doing here?"

"Your brother sent me. Told me to get working on your kitchen plumbing…"

Nice. Now she *would* have to murder her brother. And she wouldn't escape because they'd easily pin motive on her.

She turned, ignored the debris of her unfinished living room, and took the stairs two at a time. Twenty minutes later, she pulled into her parents' driveway. Samson's construction truck took up most of the space.

She took a breath. Tried to remember he was helping. Giving her a cut rate.

And inviting strange men into her home at ungodly hours.

Eve got out and headed toward the door, glancing at her watch. Not late yet, but she was cutting it close for her first day on the job in her new precinct. But a girl couldn't let life bully her—especially if it came in the form of her kid brother-slash-kitchen remodeler.

However, one step inside would rope her into breakfast, including a bright-lights-third degree interrogation about the new job. And promises to attend the annual Fourth of July barbecue.

Maybe she didn't—aw, she also had the tile issue...

The crunch of tires in the drive told her she'd hesitated too long for escape.

She turned and lifted her hand to her father, just climbing out of his truck. At least he hadn't driven the cruiser home—not anymore. The fact that he'd parked his patrol car in their suburban driveway her entire high school career had pretty much terrified and run-off every male who'd shown even the slightest interest in her. Even now, she might have to move across the country to get a date without her father doing a background check.

Frankly, even across the country, her father knew the right strings to pull. Deputy Police Inspector Danny Mulligan, twenty plus years on the job, head of the department of Violent Crimes Investigation for the city of Minneapolis knew *everybody*. Decorated, accommodated—he'd even made the papers more than a few times.

It made it difficult for a girl to slide out from under his massive shadow. His legacy had followed her right into her recent job opportunity, working for one of her father's best friends.

Chief John Booker, commander of the 5th Precinct.

And with everything inside her, she didn't want to let Booker—or her father—down.

"How's my Evie Bear," her father said, holding his arms open. At six foot, her father wasn't physically big, but he had a presence, a confidence that filled up the room. His auburn hair thinned on top, but at fifty-eight he was still lean, broad-shouldered and in shape. Nobody messed with Danny Mulligan.

"Dad, I'm twenty-six, I have a master's degree and I own my own home. It's just plain Eve."

"Not to me." He hopped up on the steps and pulled her into an embrace. "But I'll keep it Eve on the job."

"Dad—" She leaned away.

He grinned, his pale hazel-green eyes shiny with pride. "I was talking to Booker—he said you were one of his favorite crime scene rats. Can't wait to have you work for him"

"I'm a full Crime Scene Investigator now, not a rat. I'm leaving the bagging of evidence to Silas."

Her father opened the door, shooing her inside. "When are you going to date that young man? He's got a clean record—I've done my homework."

She shook her head. "He's just a friend, Dad. It would be like dating my brother."

"Evie!" Her mother came from the kitchen, wearing an apron, a pair of jeans, her dark red hair tumbling out from a headband. "I was hoping you'd stop by!" She kissed her daughter, then headed for Dad, who pulled her close. "Thank God, you're home."

Her father kissed her forehead. "Always, Bets."

Eve stepped away, into the kitchen. A year ago, her mother had declared war on the wall between the kitchen and their family room in the 1920s farmhouse—one of the original homesteads on Lake Minnetonka—and taken a sledge to the wall. To which her father and younger brother, Samson, finished demolishing, then took out the entire kitchen for a remodel.

Now, Eve grabbed a mug from the cupboard, poured herself a cup of coffee, black, then turned and stole a muffin from the plate on the long island that overlooked the family room and dining area. She paused, gazing through the massive wall of windows to the rippling blue of Lake Minnetonka. A beautiful morning, un-cluttered by clouds. Not a hint of trouble on the horizon.

If her mother hadn't been a Hubbard by birth, they wouldn't have had a hope of this view, the legacy property valued into the multi-digit millions. But Eve had only figured that out recently, during her house hunt.

She'd scored a bungalow fixer-upper in St. Louis Park with a view of the back alleyway.

But soon to have a new kitchen, starting with the tile and hopefully, running water. "Bro!" Eve directed her words toward Samson, sitting at the table nursing a cup of coffee. He wore a pair of jeans and a black T-shirt, a baseball cap on backwards, his golden brown hair poking out the back, clearly on his way to work.

"Could you please explain to me why I found a strange man in my kitchen this morning?"

Samson raised an eyebrow. "I don't know what you did last night—"

"Samson!" This from her mother. "That's not appropriate."

Samson grinned and Eve wanted to throw her muffin at him. "A plumber, okay? He shut off the water. I was in the shower."

He made a face, wrinkled his nose. "Oh, sorry. I didn't realize Chuck would be there that soon."

"Well he was, and frankly he's lucky I didn't shoot him."

"Shoot who?" her father said, coming into the room. He'd locked up his gun, toed off his shoes, and now reached for a cup of coffee.

The blood drained, just a little, from Sam's face.

"Nothing, Dad," Eve said, but walked over to the table. "However, I also found this at the scene of the crime." She reached into her bag and pulled out a sample of the tiny square sea-blue glass tiles she'd found last night in boxes on her counter. "I thought we'd talked about installing subway tile."

Samson, the inconsiderate jerk, had inherited the blue eyes of her mother, the build of their father, and enough charm that came from being the middle child to make him dangerous to her girlfriends, despite being five years younger than her. His smile contained a sort of homing beacon for trouble—hence his inability to stay in college. But he could swing a hammer, lay tile and frankly, he might have found his calling as a re-modeler.

If he could explain the tile.

"It looks better with your white cupboards, sis. All that dark wood on the island and the floor, you want something that pops, and I'm sorry, the subway tile sucks."

Huh. "When did you turn into Martha Stewart?"

Her mom set a bowl of scrambled eggs on the table. "Sit down, honey, you're just in time for breakfast."

About then, Asher shuffled in, a headset around his neck. He set his CD player on the table and slid out the chair, his curly reddish-brown hair in a mop. He wore a pair of jeans, a Guns N' Roses T-shirt, and looked ever so thrilled to be getting up at the crack of dawn for breakfast.

Eve had no sympathy for him. Asher should be used to her mother's traditions by now. Whenever their father was assigned night shift, for however long, they all trundled down for breakfast together, her mother's attempt at a regular family meal.

Of normalcy.

But nothing was ever truly normal when your dad was a cop. Every time he left the house, the unspoken ghost of fear slithered in and hovered in every conversation until he returned.

Eve would never forget the one time he didn't. The call that came, the frantic drive to the hospital. Her mother's declaration, after they'd discovered the gunshot wouldn't kill him, that none of her children could be cops.

They'd obeyed, mostly. Lucas, a lawyer, and Jake went into the Navy. Sam turned to carpentry and Asher, well it looked like he'd never get a real job, the way he played on the computer constantly. But Eve hadn't listened.

She was the one who couldn't completely escape the family instincts, and after landing a degree in biology, went into crime scene investigation, a supposed-to-be temporary job that had tunneled under her skin and found her bones.

She loved it. The dissection of a crime scene, the thorough analysis, putting the pieces together. It led her into her master's in Forensic Science.

Landed her the job for Booker.

Thankfully, Booker also hired her partner, crime scene technician Silas O'Roarke. Blond and with a quick smile, he was the guy who'd always showed up at 2 a.m. with a study pizza. They'd been friends since their college days at the University when he dropped down next to her in their 3000-level forensic anthropology class and handed her a donut. Because she looked like she needed it.

She knew Silas had picked it up at the back of the class, the first day's offerings from the professor, but the thoughtfulness... Silas was like that. As loyal as a Labrador.

And, he noticed her.

Which, when surrounded by a larger-than-life father, and handsome, football-playing brothers, seemed significant.

She slid onto the bench next to Asher. Her mother put a plate in front of her, and Eve reached for a scoopful of eggs.

"Not until we pray," her mother said, and of course, that was part of the tradition, too. Her treaty with God that everyone would return safely, one more day.

Asher turned off his music and for a moment, they were quiet. Together. Remembering Lucas in Chicago, and Jake—well, wherever he was.

The instant the prayer was over, Asher leapt for the bacon, and Eve filled her plate with eggs as her mother poured juice.

She noticed her father playing with his eggs, lost somewhere, probably on the job. He didn't usually bring it home, but a darkness stirred in his eyes.

"Rough night, Dad?" Eve asked, one eye on the time, shoveling her food in.

"We had another working girl show up dead. There's a predator out there. But I'll get him." He reached for his coffee and ran his thumb down the edge of his cup. "I just can't seem to get there fast enough. I gotta be quicker." It was a mumble more than a statement.

"No cases at the table, Danny," her mother said.

"Sorry, Bets." But he pushed his plate away. Eve got that— she'd often returned from her shift, her gut raw from what she'd seen.

"So, Eve. Now that you're over at the 5th, you get to meet the *author*." Her father said it with not a little sarcasm in his voice, and she knew exactly to whom he was referring.

Rembrandt Stone.

Famed Inspector, not only for being one of the youngest in the force, but he'd published a tell-all about his rookie year and somehow it landed on the best-seller list.

"I have a copy of *The Last Year* on my desk," she said. "It's actually good."

"Oh, please don't tell me you're a fan."

She lifted a shoulder, then glanced at Samson, who smirked, onto her game.

"Maybe I'll ask him for an autograph."

"Are you kidding me? The guy keeps a diary of his first year of training, tells a few precinct secrets and you're a fan?" He met her eyes. "There's more to Rembrandt than we know. You can't trust him—he plays by his own rules."

She took a sip of coffee. "He's cute, too."

Samson choked, coughing and put a napkin to his mouth.

Her father folded his arms over his chest. "When have you ever met Stone?"

"He played in the precinct-against-precinct softball game last summer."

And while she liked seeing her father riled, yes, Rembrandt had stood out. How could he not, with his sleeves ripped off his T-shirt, his red baseball hat shading his dark eyes. He played short-stop with the fury of a Twins starter, batted two home runs and generally took the game as seriously as a heart-attack, leading the homicide department to a ten-three win.

She'd watched from the stands, her Crime Lab team having lost the previous game to the 3rd Precinct. But it gave her the time to analyze the guy, to decide if she believed the word on the street.

That, despite his memoir, he was an enigma, a mystery. A tough nut to crack. He dated a few women, no one long term and he was a bit of a charmer. But he hung mostly with his partner, a handsome Black American man named Andrew. Both men spent time working out, too, and she could appreciate that, even from a distance.

Quite the duo, Andrew Burke and Rembrandt Stone.

They'd cracked a few beers after the game, sitting on a picnic table, greeting their fans, but Eve hadn't ventured too close.

Because she agreed with her father. Despite his memoir, she saw a recklessness behind Detective Stone's eyes, and the last thing she needed was to get wrapped up in something that could derail her career.

Besides, she didn't like troublemakers. Or the games men and women played. If a man couldn't drop the pretense, then she didn't have time or inclination to try and figure him out.

That was the problem with growing up with brothers. She was a straight-shooter, in life and in romance.

But she did like to mess with her dad.

"I watched him hit the ball, and run the bases, and...oh yeah, he's fine."

She couldn't help but smile as her father stared at her with a sort of horror.

"Okay, Eve, leave him alone." This from her mother, who was also smiling.

Eve lifted a shoulder. "Don't worry, Dad. I'm probably not even going to meet Inspector Stone. Unless we work a case together, and if so, it'll be all business."

He exhaled a visible huff of relief. "Just...don't get too close. Inspector Stone has a dark side, okay?"

She let his words bounce off her. "Speaking of my new job, I gotta run, Mom." Eve scooted her chair back and stood up. "Sam— go with the blue. But I want my water on, and no more Chuck at 6 a.m., got it?"

Samson nodded, reaching for the bacon. "You're the boss."

She grabbed a piece of bacon from the plate before Samson, then headed to the door. Climbed into her Ford Escort, a zippy, paid-for, ride. Overhead, the sky arched blue and bright, the sun early and spilling across the lake, turning it golden.

She wound her way out of the neighborhoods and toward the city. Turned on the radio. KDWB, and she sang along to Elton John's *Something About the Way You Look Tonight.*

She tapped her hand on the steering wheel and nearly didn't hear her phone buzz on the seat next to her.

She reached over for her Nokia and pressed it on. "Yeah?"

"It's me, and you need to get down to Franklin Avenue, right now."

Silas.

"Why? Did you find a dead body? Don't get started without me."

"There's maybe *five* bodies, Eve. A coffee shop blew up. We need you. It's a mess."

Shoot—and that's what she got for being irreverent of the dead. "I'm on my way."

She was hanging up when she saw smoke pluming across the downtown skyline. She dropped the phone onto the seat and got off 394 at Dunwoody, over to Lyndale, then south to Franklin.

Firetrucks jammed the streets, the air thick with spray, the odor of smoke, rubber and metal melting under the heat of the flames. She parked at a shopping center a block away, reached for her ID, hung it over her neck, grabbed her new Canon EOS-3, and got out, quick walking through the crowd.

Her heart dropped as she got closer. Where had stood a Daily Grind, one of the many coffee shops popping up around Minneapolis, now remained only a burned shell, the windows blown out into the street, the trees in the sidewalk ripped to shreds, bicycles and cars scorched, mangled.

And bodies. She counted five with body sheets draped over them, strewn in the street, not all of them intact. EMTs attended to a few victims, and an ambulance closed their doors, the sirens giving a burp before it started through the crowd. Three firetrucks sprayed their hoses on the now doused, charred skeleton of the building, but it would be an hour or more before they could get inside to assess the damage.

For now, they had to get the people back, keep anyone from touching the casualties in the street, cordon off the area to protect the evidence, and secure the site.

She found Silas standing next to a group of other CSIs. He was ungarbed, just wearing his jacket, staring at the chaos. He wore a CSI cap over his blonde hair.

"Hey."

Silas glanced at her, his mouth grim, a defeat in his pale green eyes. "Hey." He turned back to the scene. "This is rough."

A fireman carried out a child, no more than two, his body horribly burned, his light brown hair almost untouched. The man set him on the street on a body bag, pulled off his helmet and pressed the back of his hand to his mouth.

She flinched, hating the sight of a grown man crying.

Blowing out a breath, she lifted her camera and started shooting. Just to get some crowd scenes. Who knew but if it was arson, the perp could be lingering in the crowd. She kept shooting, turning—

"Hey!"

She'd bumped soundly into the man behind her. Dark hair, deep, pensive blue eyes, he wore a suit and had shaved, his dark hair wavy, a lock of it falling away, as if tempting her to reach out and curl it around her finger.

The force of his presence loosened Eve's grip on her camera and it slipped from her hands.

He caught it, his reflexes lighting fast, an almost miraculous save.

"Oh—I'm sorry!"

He handed her camera back to her. She checked it—all intact. "Thanks, wow. This is a—"

"Five thousand dollar camera. I know."

Huh. "Yeah."

He was staring at her, his mouth a little open, blue eyes latched on, his expression almost white, as if he'd seen an apparition. "It's *you*."

She raised an eyebrow. Oh. She wasn't sure what he'd heard, but, "Yeah. I'm here to work the scene. Eve Mulligan, CSI."

He took her outstretched hand, and swallowed, as if a little undone, and if she thought Rembrandt Stone could land on a calendar from fifty feet away, meeting him up close, with those blue eyes on her as if he might be drinking her in—

It sent a hot ripple right through her. No wonder they called him a lady killer. An eye-rolling nickname, but she felt her own breathing start to seize up, so there was that.

"Sorry. Uh, I'm Rem." He held out his hand. "I...wow. I forgot this part."

She frowned at him. "What part—?"

"Last—no, I mean. I had coffee before."

"Before what?" Then— oh no. "Were you in the *coffee shop*?"

"No—I mean. Yes. But not that one." He blew out a breath, his gaze landing behind her, on the carnage. "No. I was at a place called the Cuppa. It's—"

"I *love* that place. In Uptown? It's just a few blocks from my new house." Oh, and now she was babbling. Sheesh.

"I know." His eyes widened. "I mean, I know it's in Uptown."

Huh.

His hand cupped his neck. "This was supposed to play out differently."

She was starting to get a strange vibe. "Like...*how*?"

His eyes widened again and he shook his head. "Nothing."

"We have witnesses." The voice came from Inspector Andrew Burke, as he walked up to them. He shot her a smile. "Eve Mulligan. I heard you'd moved over to our precinct." He held out his hand.

She shook his hand, found it warm and solid. It seemed to calm her racing heart.

"Glad you're here," Burke said, and his gaze lifted past her, to the horror, his mouth a tight line. "C'mon. I found a woman who missed the bomb by two minutes. She's a little shaky, but she might have something that gives us a start."

Stone didn't move. Just stared at Eve, and the look on his face sent an eerie tingle through her. "I forgot how beautiful you were—*are*."

Eve just blinked at him. *What?*

And now he had Silas's attention because he'd turned.

"Oh brother," Burke said, and pulled him away.

But before he walked away, Stone stopped, looked up at the coffee shop, then back at Eve. "This time we'll catch him."

His words raised gooseflesh on her arms.

"What was that all about?" Silas said.

She watched him as he disappeared through the crowd with Inspector Burke. "I don't know. But that was weird."

"Yeah, well, I've heard stories about that guy. Trust me on this—the last thing you need is to get tangled up with him. You never know when you might end up in a book."

Stone had emerged near the sidewalk, and kneeled down next to the distraught woman. He put his hand on her shoulder, his expression softening.

Maybe. But she had the distinct impression that there was more to Rembrandt Stone. And she wouldn't mind figuring it out.

CHAPTER 6

I'm trying to focus, really, I am. On the scene, taking in the crowd, on the activity of the firefighters. And especially on the witness statement of the middle-aged woman seated on the curb, her eyes rounded as she keeps glancing at the shell of the building, still sizzling, the smoke graying the sky. I'm listening to Burke ask her the pertinents—when, where, what did she see—but frankly, I'm reeling.

Everything *feels* so real. The odor of creosote, the acrid pinch of burned metal and rubber. The wind picks up ash and blows it at our feet. The air is thick with smoke and the humidity of the firemen's spray.

The crowd is still murmuring, some people crying. Firemen are shouting, and sirens rend the air.

We interviewed her before, Laura Stoltenberg, a pretty blonde who looks like she might shatter, so I put my hand on her shoulder to keep her together. I don't offer platitudes, but Eve has told me how sometimes it's good to connect with people, to show them kindness, and while I know that, it's taken me a few years to let it out.

I give her shoulder a squeeze of comfort.

Burke glances at me when I do this, and frowns, but turns back to her.

"Do you remember the people in the shop, anyone who might have looked out of place? Or was acting suspiciously?"

Bombings are still rare in 1997. It's been two years since the Oklahoma bombing, only a year since the Olympic Park bombing in Atlanta, and it's the current thinking that bombings are personal, that the perpetrator has a political agenda against this particular store. But in the twenty years since, I know that they can be as unpredictable as the weather in Minnesota. People choosing random places to make a point.

Of course, this is fourteen years before 9/11 and that was hardly random, so maybe things haven't changed that much. And, my memory of two more bombings of coffee shops reminds me that there is a connection we never solved.

Not the first time.

Although, again, I don't have a clue what is happening here. If it's a dream, it feels painfully real. But like always, in every dream, I want to change things. And in the back of my mind, I'm hit with the crazy thought that if I can solve the crime, I might finally put a lid on my nightmares.

It's a long shot, but as dreams, or nightmares go, this is the mother lode, so it has to mean *something*.

I'm not sure when I'll wake up, but until I do, I have routines, habits, and a job that keeps me pinned to the moment.

"I don't know," Laurie says. "I stood in line like everyone else, trying to understand the menu. I only just heard of this place. I visited a Starbucks in Seattle, and I thought…" She shook her head. "Why would someone blow up a *coffee* shop?"

It hits me then that coffee mania is just beginning to hit the nation.

"Okay, Mrs. Stoltenburg, we'll call you if we have any further questions." Burke is helping her to her feet.

My gaze, of course, returns to Eve. She's wearing her kinky, beautiful auburn hair down, the way I like it, and it looks like she's let it air dry. I love her curls. It's the one thing about her I always notice—how she wears her hair. Down, straightened, up, it has an allure to it I find fascinating.

That, and her eyes, green, with crazy amber highlights and yeah, I'm being poetic, but let's not forget I'm a writer, or trying to be. I'm supposed to notice those things.

Let's face it, everything about Eve can level me. Funny that only just last night we were talking about how we met. If I hadn't slammed into Burke at the Cuppa, dousing him with the vanilla latte (he pulled out a clean shirt from the trunk of his car, of course), I would have repeated the past, the dream I can never seem to escape.

Until now.

In the standard version of my dream-slash-past, my coffee would have drenched her, she would have dropped her camera.

And—*oh crap*—I would have had a reason to see her again, to show up in her office with an apology coffee and an offer to buy her a new camera.

Instead, not only did I catch the camera, but I want to cringe at the words I now hear replaying in my brain. *I forgot how beautiful you were—are.*

Shoot, why didn't I keep my mouth closed? This is why I never really dated long term. Because I wear my heart on my sleeve and frankly, my words get me into trouble.

Eve was the only one who could plow through my impulsiveness, my stupid words, to hear what I was really trying to say.

Truth is, I do better with the written word. Until recently, apparently, if the blank pages on my laptop are any indication.

The fire is out, and the guys in turnout gear are doing a walkthrough, testing the place for hot spots. The EMTs and paramedics have triaged the victims and Eve and her crew are taping off the area for the evidence collection to begin.

Eve shoots pictures, directs traffic. She doesn't know it yet but she's about to become a legend in our department for her ability to dissect and analyze the scene, to piece together the evidence, and aid me in solving crimes.

We're about to become a team that will last for the next ten years before we make it permanent.

Burke has left me—I didn't notice that—but now he's walking back, holding the little notebook that he'll soon replace with a tape recorder. And eventually, his smart phone. Burke is into technology that way.

I try to put myself back in the game and scramble to say something halfway intelligent. "There's a pretty big crowd here. Let's make sure we talk to everybody." Who knows but key witnesses might have slipped away last time.

I talk like a man who is not caught in a dream, but the actual past. Like I'm not going to wake up any moment, a scream on my lips, my body covered in sweat.

"I interviewed a man on a bicycle who was riding past," Burke says. "He didn't see anyone standing outside, watching the place. And I talked to the fire chief. He can't be sure—they'll get the arson guys out here, but he says the blast looks like it originated from inside the building, as opposed to one of these charred cars. I've got officers talking to other witnesses."

I know all this, but I nod, because I'm not sure if I'm supposed to let on that I know it. If it's a dream, does it matter? Maybe I should simply mention that we need to track down the next location, camp out and wait.

But for whom?

Burke. He doesn't seem any different than twenty years ago. Sure, he has hair now, but when it comes to investigations, he's still the all-business, let's-get-it-done guy who follows every rule, crosses every T.

Me, I'm more of an instinct fella, and right now I'm scanning the crowd. Because I've always felt like the bomber was a voyeur— that he stuck around to watch his handiwork. In fact, there was evidence the bomb was on a clock, a situation that gave him time to find the perfect location.

Eve is taking pictures of the crowd. That fact lodges in my brain and sticks there. I know she took pictures before, but the bombings happened so fast—three within forty-eight hours—we didn't have them developed in time to use them. CSI barely had the evidence bagged from the first, only a few of the families notified when the second happened—tomorrow morning, early.

I can't remember exactly where. I know it's in the Uptown area, but it's not a Daily Grind.

I'm wracking my brain for the place when I spot John Booker.

The sight of him turns my mouth dry. He's exactly how I remember. And he's heading my direction.

It's always been my contention that Booker was born a century too late. He reminds me more of a gunslinger than a detective, the way he sizes up a man before he speaks. He doesn't look like a cowboy, not dressed in his uniform; it's more the sense of him, the aura of the long arm of the law reaching out to strangle the truth from you.

He's tall, solidly built, keeps a regular appointment with his barber for his graying brown hair, stands six foot four, and although no man has ever scared me, a stare from John Booker's gray eyes comes close.

He finds me and I am shaken with a strange rush of emotion. Wow, I miss him.

"You're lead on this, Rem."

This ancient, pivotal conversation is slowly coming back to me. I try and act surprised. "Why?"

"Because you're ready—you and Burke. Run your investigation by me and I'll give you my input, but we gotta find whoever did this, and fast before the city freaks out."

Not to mention, stop the next one. I'm seriously debating adding that, but I'm not sure if that will emerge quite the way I intend it.

I might get a look from John like I did from Eve. The one that suggests I didn't make a stellar first impression.

But, yes, this time, we'll catch him. I make that promise to myself and, in an amended version, to John who nods and walks back to the horror.

I take a breath, keenly aware that I'm back to the beginning.

And this time, at least in my dreams, everything will be different.

CHAPTER 7

I can't shake this eerie voodoo. It isn't quite like déjà vu, but close enough, the hiccup inside that says you've said that, seen that, heard that, done that before. And you *have*, it's just…

I just burned my mouth on the bitter, too hot coffee.

You don't dream that, do you? The fatness of your tongue as it absorbs the heat?

Or the way it burns my hand as I jerk back, the liquid sloshing over the edge of my Styrofoam cup.

Burke looks over at me, frowns. We're standing in the community room of the shiny new 3rd Precinct, with the bullet proof, floor to ceiling windows that overlook 31st Street. Our usual haunt, located downtown in the ancient City Hall building, is under renovation. Along one wall of the community room, I've pinned all the faces of the deceased, some of them already identified. Seven total. Two of them are men, who carried their identification with them. The rest are women. And one toddler. I grit my teeth.

Melinda Jorgensen is the third picture in, on the top row. She hasn't yet been named, and it's a gut punch to see the word "unidentified" next to her picture. Down below, on the bottom is her towheaded son, and with everything inside me I want to unpin him, place him next to his mother.

Weird, I know.

Everything about this is weird, though, right? In the gathering crowd, I recognize faces, men I haven't worked with in years. Including Jim Williams, the beat cop who I lost—will lose?—my job over in about seventeen years. And in the far corner, in the back, Inspector Danny Mulligan, who's come over from downtown to help us sort this out.

It's exactly like seeing a ghost. Danny, Eve's dad, along with her brother, Ash, were murdered just a few weeks after we met. A Fourth of July shooting that forever shut down that holiday for us. We never shoot off fireworks, never barbecue hot dogs.

I caught Danny's gaze on me today as I walked in, as if sizing me up. I don't remember that from before, but maybe I'm not as shook up this time around.

Or maybe I just know that all this chatter won't matter. Not unless it leads to a perp in the next sixteen hours.

We've interviewed twelve witnesses, just Burke and I, and I've outsourced the rest of the interviews to others in my department. None of the witnesses, so far, saw anything unusual, but this is before the if-you-see-something, say-something era, so no one is actually looking.

Wow, we thought we were safe back then. Or now. Whatever.

I'm standing off to the side, holding up a wall with my shoulder while the fire chief gives us an update. On the overhead is a diagram of the attack, and Dayton is drawing on the view film, indicating the preliminary scene reports.

"The arson investigators will confirm, but we believe the blast came from inside the shop." He points to the layout of the store.

"Given the damage to the front of the store, the bomb was probably placed near the brewed coffee machines."

He draws a line across one side of the store. "There was a row of help-yourself coffee thermoses here, with overflow under the counter. The current theory is that one of those might have been a decoy."

"And housed the bomb?" Burke asks. "So, how did the bomber get it there?"

"Could have been someone who works there," says Danny from the back where he's standing, his arms folded and hands tucked under his armpits. He's radiating a sort of fury fed by the energy in the room. We're all angry, and getting more so with every victim identification. "Maybe a disgruntled employee?"

"We're running down the backgrounds of all the current employees, but it would need to be someone who knew explosives, like a Gulf War veteran, perhaps?" Booker interjects this from his position near the windows.

We tracked down every surviving employee over the course of the year after the final bombing—no one had the background that Booker is suggesting, but maybe we missed something, so I stay silent.

However, I'm antsy, because none of this conversation hastens the suspicion that the bomber was on a timer. That he might have been nearby.

We don't know to look at the…photographs. *The photographs Eve took.* This time, we can get them developed.

"This is taking too long," I say under my breath to Burke. I dump my coffee in the trash bin and am pushing out the nearby door when I hear Burke stifle a word and fall in behind me.

We're out in the hallway when he grabs my arm. "Where are you going?"

Because this is just a dream—a very rich, vivid dream, for sure, but a dream nonetheless, I say, "We're running out of time. There's another bomb out there, and we have to find it."

Burke's mouth opens, and he stares at me like I've just told him the Vikings are going to win the Super Bowl.

Burke drags me toward the men's room. He pushes me inside, and I sort of bounce off the tile, rounding on him fast. "What's your problem?"

"What's *yours?*" Burke says. "You're running this investigation, but instead of helming it, it's like your mind is somewhere else. And I'm starting to figure out where. Did you get a tip that you're not sharing with the rest of us? About another bombing? Why are you keeping the rest of us in the dark? A toddler died, Rem. If you know something—"

"Step back." I give him a shove. "I don't know anything." Which, frankly, isn't a lie. We just didn't get that far into the investigation before the trail went cold, just like that, nothing else to go on.

We have stop him this time, because I can't wake up to another case gone frigid. "I just…I have a hunch, okay?"

Burke's eyes narrow.

And that's when I get a glimpse of myself in the mirror.

You've gotta be kidding me.

I'm staring at the twenty-eight-year-old version of myself.

A very young, bright-eyed, and way-too-confident version, thanks to my New York Times bestseller run. My hair is shaggy and top-heavy, with a oh-so-90s lock over my face. I'm wearing a black suit jacket and a white shirt, but my tie—it's wide, red and it has baseballs on it. Whose idea was this? Yeah, probably mine, but Burke is wearing a normal gray, striped number that I barely noticed.

I rip off the tie and shove it in the trash, but the next thing I notice is…I have my body back. The one I spent way too much time honing.

I liked this body.

And, I very much like this dream.

Especially the second chance I'm getting. I turn to Burke. "I just have a hunch that this is only the first bomb. And that maybe the bomber was in the crowd, watching." I close my eyes for a second. "I need to talk to Eve."

Burke is frowning. I still can't get over that hair. Or that stupid soul patch.

"Eve?"

"Eve Mulligan, the CSI at today's scene? She was snapping pictures—"

"The redhead? Danny Mulligan's daughter?"

Yeah, the redhead. And if Eve heard Burke call her that, he'd be so very dead.

Burke is shaking his head. "You'd better stay away from that one, Rem."

I don't know why, but a spurt of cockiness makes me say, "Naw. I'm going to marry her." Well, it's true, isn't it?

Burke stares at me like I've taken a hit too hard. "Right. Okay, Rem, whatever you say."

I push past him. Because I've just come up with a reason to see her. And a way to stop bombing number two. I'll get the photos, go to the next scene and simply stake it out. Wait.

Stop the carnage and get the bomber.

Unless, of course, I wake up first.

So, right now, I'm sloughing off the eerie voodoo of this dream and diving in, tasting the sweet sense of justice, of triumph.

While I'm stopping the crime of the decade, maybe I'll also take this body for a spin at the gym, one more time. Climb into the ring with Burke, now that I know his moves. I hide a smile, wishing on stars that whatever took me down and into this dream has me out for a long winter's nap.

"I'm going over to the crime lab to see if Eve has downloaded her pictures—"

"Downloaded?"

"Uh … developed. But first, I'm going back to the Cuppa. I need a white mocha with a berry shot."

"A what?"

I try not to smile. "It's coffee. Like an upgraded latte." Oh, the nineties. "Don't you watch *Friends*? Man, I forgot how sheltered you are. You need to live larger, dude."

"Hey—"

I grin, because I'm seeing the Burke I knew, and our friendship is still intact, the sparring fun, the laughter easy. Back when he didn't consider me a traitor.

"Take a breath, Burke. I'll text you if I find anything."

The frown is back on Burke's face. Deeper this time.

I push past him, unbuttoning the collar of my shirt at the neck as I leave the restroom.

"I'm coming with you," Burke says, on my heel.

I turn, walking backwards. "Actually, you're not. I need to talk to Eve alone. You go back in there. Tell Booker I've got a lead. And keep an eye on Danny Mulligan."

Burke stops in the middle of the hallway. "Stay away from her."

"Not a chance." I turn back just in time to hit the door, and find myself outside, in the glaring hot sun. A couple of Rollerbladers skate by, along with a car pumping out Puff Daddy's "Bad Boys for Life."

Funny how songs come back to you, as if they'd just been tucked away on a shelf.

I head around back to the lot and stand in the middle of the pavement, searching.

My car isn't here. Sure, I rode in with Burke, in his Acura Integra, but I thought for sure I'd left the Porsche at the station.

I turn, baffled and I see Burke come out. I ignore the fact that he's ignored *me*, and say, "Where's my 911?"

He raises an eyebrow. "I hope, in the junkyard, where it belongs."

Huh? "It's…" Not yet repaired. Because now I remember. At the time of the bombing, I'd parked the car in my father's garage, on his hobby farm out in Waconia, because I live in a one bedroom apartment four blocks off the lake, in a three-story walk up brownstone on Holmes.

It's vintage, has some charm with its wood floors and ancient knocking radiators, but mostly was a cheap place in the city I could rent back before the book sales started adding to my nest egg.

Actually, the entire place needs a remodel, but I only know that now.

I currently drive a…that's right, a 1984 Camaro and something inside me ignites when I see my first love waiting for me in a spot near the edge where no one can hurt her.

I head toward her, but Burke catches up to me. "Listen—I don't know why you're acting so weird, but Booker wants to see you. Says it's urgent."

Shoot. But in this dream, I still work for him so I route back inside and find him sitting in his office. Mulligan and a couple other precinct investigators shuffle out. Danny gives me the dark eye, but I ignore him and poke my head in. "You wanted to see me, Boss?"

He frowns, and maybe I haven't started calling him that, yet. "Come in, Rembrandt. Shut the door."

Hmm.

He gets up, and gestures to me to sit down, which is a little weird, but I do, on the sofa shoved against the wall.

He leans against the desk and blows out a breath. "Okay, I got some news, and I know it might be just another dead lead, but..."

The way he's acting, the grim look...oh, no, in all the bombing clutter I'd *forgotten*—

"A fisherman found a dead body a couple days ago over in Swan Lake, out in Waconia. They hauled it in and sent it to the M.E's office. I got a call this morning—it's on the machine."

He's reaching over to play it for me, but I know what it says. My body goes numb.

"It's my brother."

Suddenly, I desperately want to wake up. Because I remember this part of my past too. The fact that I was so busy with the bombings that someone else went to talk to my parents.

Someone else, not their detective son, who'd become a Inspector for exactly this reason—to find my brother.

I should have been there when they got the news.

I will be, this time.

"It's not for sure. It takes a while to get back the DNA evidence, but it was a kid, and there was a backpack..."

"It's a Return of the Jedi pack, isn't it?"

He nods and while I know it's coming, the gesture hits me like a fist.

"I just thought I should give you a heads up. I know the timing stinks—"

"I'll tell my parents." I get up.

"It's not conclusive yet," he says. "Wait until the DNA comes back. But…I'm really sorry, Rembrandt. I know that you probably knew he was dead, but there's always that hope, right?"

I shake my head. "There are no happy endings, boss. I'm used to it."

The words dig in and now I'm annoyed and frustrated as I head back out into the heat. If I really could dream myself into the past and make some changes, I'd start with the day my brother went missing.

The day I left him behind.

Burke is waiting for me, leaning on his car, his arms folded as I come out. "You in trouble?"

"No," I snap. But, he doesn't deserve that, so I add, "Chief just wanted to talk to me about an old case."

He nods and follows me over to my car. Only then do I notice the flattened back tire. Really?

I give it a kick. "When did this happen?"

"Last night. I gave you a ride home. Remember?"

No, I want to say. Because yesterday was twenty-four freakin' years ago, and even in my subconscious I don't have that kind of memory.

But that accounts for why he picked me up this morning.

I pop the trunk and find my jack kit and tire in the back. Taking off my coat, I set to work, and twenty minutes later, the spare is on.

"Can you follow me to the garage? There's Speedy's off Lake, and Rusty will have me back in action in a couple hours."

He's about seventy-four now in my time, and we're still good friends. I throw the tire in the back, close the trunk.

"Yeah. Sure."

I dust off my hands. "Then we need to get a list of every coffee shop in the Minneapolis metro area."

"What are we going to do, stake out every single one?" Burke raises an eyebrow.

"If I have to."

"That's some hunch, pal. I hope you're right." Burke stalks over to his car.

I slide into the sweet leather of my Camaro, roll down the window, start her up, and the stereo kicks in. My play list, at least, hasn't changed in years.

I pull out to Boston's, "More Than a Feeling."

CHAPTER 8

Eight hours on the job and Eve just wanted to go home and climb into her tub, (if she had water) and hide under a mound of bubbles.

Wash the odor of smoke and ash, burned rubber, and soggy cinders from her body.

Feed the beast growling in the pit of her gut, and if she were honest, she could really go for a cup of—

"Coffee?"

The voice made her look up from the table, where she was sketching a rough diagram of the coffee shop, scene labeling the various areas from where they'd gathered bomb debris and recovered bodies. She'd use it later to possibly create a reproduction of the event. Help detectives like the one standing in front of her figure out who was behind this horrific crime.

Her gaze went to the proffered coffee, then back to Inspector Stone. He wore a look of expectancy on his face.

"I drink tea."

"No, you don't. You love coffee. And you're going to love this. It's a vanilla mocha with a shot of raspberry. It's like candy. Trust me on this."

He raised one dark eyebrow and admittedly, her heart gave a little start.

He was better looking than his book jacket. Especially with his collar unbuttoned, the tiniest grizzle of whiskers across his chin. Those blue eyes skimmed over her, checking her out.

Interesting.

He came back to her gaze with a smirk. Like she should fall at his feet to his offer of coffee.

"What are you doing here?" she asked, not showing a hoot of interest in the coffee.

They were working off site from the crime scene lab, in a warehouse they sometimes used to process and catalog all the evidence.

Silas and other crime scene techs were sorting evidence bags—clothing, pieces of the store, items that looked like bomb casings.

His smirk vanished. "I need your help. What can you tell me?"

She raised an eyebrow at his sudden honesty and took the coffee. "We're just getting started. If we can isolate the bomb casing in the next forty-eight hours, it'll be a miracle. The best I can do for you is to focus on the makeup of the explosive residue, see if I can get a signature mix. Bomb makers are artists, and they tend to have a signature."

She took a sip of the coffee. Shoot, that *was* good—a hint of raspberry? And vanilla? "What's in this?"

"Mocha. Raspberry. Vanilla. Told you that you'd like it."

He had a nice smile. It lit up his eyes, added a dangerous charm to them. So there were at least two layers to Mr. Rembrandt

Stone—smolder on his book cover, charming in real life. Interesting.

"Listen," she said. "We'll find it—but it'll take time."

"Which we don't have. I think the bomber was in the crowd today."

She put the coffee down. "What makes you say that?"

"Just…a hunch. But I also think this isn't the last bomb."

His words put a fist in her. "What are you saying?"

"I think he's going to do it again. And soon. Very soon."

"Why?"

"I don't know…" He looked away, then back to her. "It's just…a gut feeling. I think he's trying to make a point, and it's not quite made yet." His lips tightened into a grim line.

Layer number three. The guy really cared.

Unfortunately, "I don't know how I can help you."

"The shots you took today—are they developed yet?"

She'd filled up three rolls of her 35mm film taking shots of the crowd, then the scene. She'd handed off her camera to one of the techs and they'd continued shooting every piece of evidence. "I think we have about fifteen rolls of film."

"I just need the crowd shots."

"Because you think you can spot him—or her, although bombers tend to be male—in the photos? How will you know who you're looking for?"

He lifted a shoulder.

"Wait, please don't say it's a gut feeling."

He smiled. "Okay."

She sighed, glancing over at Silas and the crew. He was watching her, his pale green eyes not missing a thing.

She turned back to Rembrandt. "This isn't the order we do things in, Inspector. You don't even know what you're looking for."

"I know. And I know I'm jumping ahead, but…please?"

It was the *please* that did it. So different from the weird, almost invasive man she'd met earlier today, this man had a sweet humility about him.

Shoot, she liked him. And then there was the coffee.

"Okay. But we'll have to go to the Forensic Photography services at the lab downtown."

Rembrandt gave a slight nod. "Burke will drive."

She grabbed the camera, the rolls of film, her bag, and followed him out to the lot. Andrew Burke was leaning against his car, waiting, handsome to the bone.

"Hi again, Detective Burke," she said.

He glanced at Rembrandt. "Apparently he can't stop harassing you today. Just Burke is fine."

She slid into the backseat of his Integra. "We're going to the photo lab."

"Have you come up with any theories so far?" Burke asked as he pulled out. Rembrandt sat in the other seat, in front.

"Just that we think the blast came from one of the coffee canisters, given the pattern. It's concentrated on one side of the building, although everyone sitting in the eating area was killed. Terrible."

Rembrandt stared out the window, his hand rubbing his watch, his thumb moving over the face. A nervous habit, probably.

"Rough first day," Burke said.

She shrugged. "I just want to make sure we don't miss anything. Let this guy slip away. Not catching him isn't something I want to think about."

Rembrandt drew in a long breath and nodded without looking at her.

They worked their way into the city, the sun low as it spilled over streets and along the paved sidewalks. Burke pulled up in front of the massive, city-block wide municipal building. "I'll park and catch up with you."

"Third floor," Eve said and followed Rembrandt up the wide front steps.

She always felt as if she might be walking back into history every time she entered the circa 1887, Romanesque building. Its thick granite walls kept the air cool despite the early June heat, the rotunda soaring fifteen stories. Inside, carved pillars encased the ancient elevators, and the huge room was centered by a marble statue of a man leaning against a paddle wheel of a riverboat, holding a cornstalk.

Stone led the way across the marble floor, then up the wide staircase. She almost had to run to catch up.

"You okay?" She didn't know why, because she hardly knew him, but he appeared rattled. Or maybe that was just his driven personality.

He seemed to almost have forgotten her, because he turned then, his hand on the rail, and nodded. "I think so."

Huh. "We'll find him, Inspector." He made a sort of grunt of agreement, deep in his chest.

The photo lab was located on the third floor, behind one of the original wooden doors. She greeted a couple familiar faces, then headed toward the dark room. "I'll need to process these films. If you want to come back—"

"I'm staying right here." He reached for the film, which she'd dumped onto a table. "Which one of these is it?"

"The canister labeled number one." She plucked it from his hand. "I really don't need help."

"I know that, Eve."

83

But he didn't move away.

"Are you going to be like this for every case?"

"Probably, although I promise, I'll grow on you."

"Like a wart?" She walked into the dark room, and he followed. But she heard a huff that sounded a lot like a chuckle.

She flicked on the purple light, waited for him to close the door, then took the film picker and tugged the film from the cartridge. "This shouldn't take too long. We just got a new developing machine."

He stood with his back to the door, blocking it, as if afraid someone might come in. "There's a little light that tells people we're in here. And it locks from the inside."

He'd taken on a purply hue, looking downright sinister standing there.

"So, what's your story, Inspector?" She cut the film square, then taped it to a plastic leader card.

"I wrote my story," he said. "Didn't you read it?"

Every page, cover to cover. "Naw. I'm not a reader."

Silence and when she glanced at him, one side of his mouth had quirked up. "Mmmhmm."

She frowned. "Okay. I read parts. I like the story of how you found the murderer of the old dentist through the killer's bite marks."

"Yeah. It was a burglary gone wrong. The dentist surprised the perp, they got into a struggle, and he bit the dentist. We nailed the guy from the bite marks on the dentist's arm—right there in his files."

"Clever." She printed out a sticker with the identification marker and pasted it to the film.

"Thanks."

"I'm surprised how many cases you solved your rookie year, actually. You're like a dog with a bone."

He laughed then, a rumble that slid under her skin, sank into her soul.

"What?" She opened the machine and stuck the leader card in.

"Nothing." He had folded his arms, was shaking his head, still wearing a slight smile. Apparently laughing at his own private joke.

"Your book didn't say why you joined the force."

She didn't even have to see it. She felt it. A wall going up. She'd probed too far. His smile faded as the machine began processing the film. He ducked his head, his hands going to his pockets.

Silence labored between them as she stared at the machine. Watching the developer phase, the bleaching, then fixing, then washing.

She fully expected a full-out stiff arm, a shutdown of their conversation but after a long, deep sigh, Rembrandt Stone began speaking softly.

"When I was twelve, my brother was kidnapped while we were out riding our bikes. They…they think they've just found his body. It's been sixteen years. Not knowing."

Everything shut down with his words, and she stared at him. "Oh my."

He looked up, met her eyes, a sorrow in them despite the darkness that reached inside, unsettled her.

"I can't get past the idea I could have stopped it. Mickey was way behind me, around a bend in the road, and I saw this white van drive by. We were on a remote dirt road—no reason for that van to be there, and I had this weird sting in my gut. When I discovered he wasn't following, I went back to find him and found his bike on the side of the road. He'd vanished."

"The police—?"

"Scoured the area for days, weeks. My parents never stopped looking." He drew in a breath, and seemed to be about to add more, but then simply shrugged and looked away.

"I'm so sorry, Inspector."

"Rem," he said, looking up. "I'd like us to be friends."

Oh, and what was she supposed to do with that? Because she'd never met a man who cut right past the charades and showed up with the truth. A man without games or a hidden agenda, no secrets.

It only made her painfully aware of how much she suddenly wanted to know more about him, the layers yet unseen.

The photo development had moved to stabilizing, a chemical process that uniformly dried the film, set the image permanently.

"So, my guess is that you became a detective to find your brother?"

"I couldn't save my brother, and we never found his killer. If I can protect other people from that kind of pain, I will."

"I get it." She nodded. "I had a friend who was killed by a hit and run driver when I was thirteen. I always had this hunch she knew the person who killed her. But what did I know? I was a kid. And it might have been my overactive imagination."

"Or, not. Maybe it was the budding investigator in you."

"Or, it could have been my favorite Alfred Hitchcock mystery series going to my head."

"Jupiter Jones, Bob Andrews, and Pete Crenshaw. I loved those books. I didn't know you read those. Wow." He sounded genuinely, oddly surprised.

Didn't know? Why would he? Maybe it was just an expression. "I loved them. That and Encyclopedia Brown, and not a few Hardy Boys."

"Nancy Drew?"

"The complete collection."

"Hang onto them. The original books will be collector's items someday."

The film had finished processing and the machine churned it back out. She cut the strip and hung it on a tree. "Now it just has to dry. Then we'll put it through the scanning mask and turn these negatives into positives."

He wore a smile again, something warm and sweet, as if she'd said something clever.

"What?"

"You need to eat. Your stomach is growling."

Oh. It had, but— "I'm fine."

"You're going to get all grouchy and frustrated. Listen, we're not far from the Towne Hall Brewery. You love—I mean, you're going to love the pretzels there. Beer cheese queso."

"Maybe I'll just have a salad."

"We'll see." He was wearing the smirk again.

She considered him, feeling a weird tug to say yes. As if it was already a foregone conclusion that she'd not only have dinner with this man, but like he said, they'd become friends.

Still, they had a job to do. "We have about an hour before this is ready to run through the scanning mask…"

"Trust me, we're coming back, Eve. He's not getting away with this…not on my watch."

A sudden darkness shifted into his eyes, almost a controlled rage and it spiraled down inside her, took hold.

She couldn't shake the bone deep idea that Rembrandt Stone was oh, so much more than the cover of his book, that he meant his words, kept promises, and would track down the perpetrator of this terrible act.

"Okay, Inspector," she said. And as they left, as they found Burke, waiting for them in the lobby, she made one promise to herself.

She would not let herself fall for Rembrandt Stone.

CHAPTER 9

I am cheating.

And I don't care.

I'm sitting in the original, not-overhauled location of one of our—Eve and my—favorite haunts. We only found the pub a few years ago, after the remodel, so seeing the vintage brick walls, the arches behind the mirrored bar, the scuffed wooden floors, and the hanging lantern lights has me in a nostalgic mood.

Zepplin plays through the 90s-sized speakers in the four corners of the pub and I tap my fingers on the wooden table watching Eve as she tears apart her pretzel, one bite at a time, eying me with a smile.

I grin. "I know, right?"

I order a lager—an early version of what will later be award-winning, but is still today, monumental. I probably shouldn't be drinking on the job, but this is a dream, right?

Besides, Burke has always been the stickler, and nurses a Diet Coke to go with his bratwurst—my suggestion by the way because I know how he's going to become an addict.

Eve picks up a napkin, wipes her mouth. "Okay, true confession. I read your book."

I don't know why this old information warms me to my core, but something about her admission makes me want to be the guy she will someday believe in.

"And?"

"My dad hated it, although I don't think he even read it. I've never seen a copy at the house."

I'm not surprised by this, but this is fresh news, actually. Remember, I never got to know Danny Mulligan, but I would have liked to. He had a reputation as a good cop, the kind of guy you wanted backing you up. I would've liked him to like the book. And, me. "Why does he hate it?"

"He says you gave away secrets, the kind of things only cops know. That you can't be trusted." She's sizing me up, testing me.

I've always liked that about Eve—she's a straight shooter, doesn't mince words. It's also the reason why I never let her do the talking when we happened to question witnesses together. It's good to play a few games, and she hates them.

I frown at her words. "Your dad is wrong. If he'd read my book, he'd know I didn't betray anybody. It was my story to tell. And I was careful. I didn't give away any secrets. You *can* trust me, Eve." I meet her eyes now, because I really need her to believe this.

She nods, as if taking in my words. "So, why? Whatever possessed you to write a book?"

I feel a sort of freedom in my answer, one that comes with impunity. It's not like I'm going to wake up tomorrow with a hangover, regretting the previous night.

In other words, it's my dream, so I'll do what I want.

I take a gulp of my beer, wipe the foam from my mouth. "I started it as a journal. Just my thoughts, my daily activities. A place to sort it all out, you know?"

"Sort what out? Life?"

I lift a shoulder. "Why, maybe. The reasons people do what they do. Maybe I was looking for insight." I lean forward. "Or to learn from my mistakes."

"You had an extraordinary amount of collars for a rookie detective." Her pretty eyes are on me and Burke raises an eyebrow at me, even as he's sopping up his fries with ketchup.

"I got lucky. And smarter, perhaps."

Burke chuckles. "No, let's just stay with lucky."

"Instincts, Burke. That's what it's called." I reach over and snag a fry.

"It's a good book," Eve says finally. "Unguarded."

I'm not sure what to do with that. Reviewers called it "gritty, honest, and a raw portrayal of the darker side of crime." I stay silent.

She is back to tearing her pretzel. "That story of the little girl who went missing."

Yeah, I remember, because for a long time I couldn't shake the echo of our own dark years after Mickey vanished. Age four, she went missing from Minnehaha Park while on a family picnic. We searched for days, with dogs and local volunteers. She was found not at the park but ninety minutes north, near a wilderness park in Little Falls. She'd been taken by a coworker of the mother's.

I nod. "It was a passing comment from the father, during the initial interview that caught my attention. Something about his wife talking to a friend. We tracked down the friend, put a name to him and linked him to a truck spotted at the crime scene."

"And arrested him back at his job," Eve says, her gaze holding mine.

Okay, despite the dream, my throat is thick because I wrote about it—not just the case, but the anger that gnawed in my gut for weeks afterward. The nights I roamed the house, or haunted the gym. Maybe those were the secrets Mulligan hated revealed.

I did leave a few things out, however, and I look away. There's a reason a guy like me can't believe in happy endings.

All we can hope for are endings we might, somehow, survive.

"I remember that case," Burke says, reaching for a napkin. "Rem didn't sleep for three days while we hunted for her."

I lift a shoulder, but really, how could I? Not with Mickey a ghost in my head. "I promised the family answers."

"You promise everyone answers," Burke says, crumpling the napkin and tossing it into the middle of the table. "Someday you're going to make promises you can't keep."

He has no idea. I sigh. "Listen, answers are all they have left. Their lives are permanently shattered and there's no coming back. If I give them answers, then maybe they can stop hoping and start figuring out how to live with the wreckage of their lives."

I hear my own jaded history in my words, the fact my parents spent the better part of their lives holding onto a barren hope. I'm not sure why I let this spill out, maybe remnants of the frustration of my waking life, the fact that I still haven't mended from my own jagged pieces. Maybe you never do, really. Maybe, when tragedy hits, all you have left is the broken shards of happiness.

My sudden morose comment has pushed silence between us, stolen the magic from the dream.

As is her nature, Eve rescues me. "That's why I became a CSI. Answers." She offers me a smile. "We'll find the bomber, Rem."

I nod, the image of Melinda Jorgenson and her son suddenly in my head.

And, she called me Rem. Nice. We're making progress.

She grabs a napkin and wipes off her fingers. "I think I'll get my father your book for Christmas. Maybe you could sign it for me." She grins, and something about it strikes me as different, odd. Whole, unreserved.

It makes me, ache, suddenly, to see it. Because I really miss that smile, the one without the fractures.

If I could stop her father and brother's murders, that would also be on my list of items to revisit. Another dream for another day, perhaps.

"No problem," I say.

Her cell phone rings and she pulls out an ancient, but probably fairly new, Nokia, presses it on. "This is Eve."

By her wince, the way her fingers go to her nose, pinching the bridge, I immediately want to leap in and fix whatever the problem is.

Habits.

"Okay, fine Sams. Just get the water on as soon as you can…"

Samson, her younger brother. He's a big real estate mogul now, but he started out working with his hands. He comes over every now and again and gives me grief about my meager remodeling skills, which frankly aren't that terrible.

I remember the wretched job he did on her kitchen in that tiny bungalow. Those terrible ice-blue tiles—wait, she must be mid-remodel right now. And, if I'm reading the conversation clues right, without plumbing.

I'm barely stopping myself from offering her the use of my place, because I really do know better, but see, I also know…well, my wife. And how she loves her nightly baths. And more than that, seeing her young, and pretty and without the grief and worry and years and years of frustration that I'm about to put her through...

I'd like to skip that part, please. Get right to the moment I come to my senses and propose. But that's a good decade from now, so...

Except, this is a dream, right? I can do what I want.

"Yeah, I was there. It was bad." Her conversation has switched direction, and she glances at me. She's talking about the bombing. "I can't discuss the case, Sams—fine. No, I don't think it was political. Why would it be? It was a *coffee* shop."

She's frowning.

Samson, for all his brawn, started out with a philosophy degree, and has spent most of his life exploring the planet, when he isn't installing reclaimed wood in new suburban kitchens. Two years ago, he hiked Machu Picchu, and before that spent a summer in the Borneo rainforest working on a clean water project. Eve has always thought it's his way of living Asher's dreams.

But his question has my ears perking up. We never nailed down a motive for the bombings. I file it away however when she hangs up, returning to my previous thought.

"You're out of water?"

She nods, then shakes her head. "I bought this cute bungalow off—

Webster Ave South.

I nearly say it, but something inside me cuts me off. A weird gut feeling I can't put a name to.

"Webster and Lake. It was built in 1941, so the plumbing is archaic. I don't know why I agreed to a full-on remodel, but—"

"You like a challenge," I say quietly, smiling.

She meets my eyes, something playful in them that I like.

Burke is rolling his eyes. He's finished with his brat and I'm guessing the photos have processed by now, so I signal to the waiter for the check.

We're back in the photo lab thirty minutes later and Eve lays out the pictures on a massive work table. "Which ones do you want enlarged?"

I lean over her, aware that she smells good for a woman without a shower, and point to the twenty or so of the crowd.

Meanwhile, I've asked Burke to get that list of coffee shops together because I've been wracking my brain for hours and I still can't pull up the location of the second bombing.

While my subconscious tracks it down inside my dream, I'll drive around, maybe help the memory surface. Once I find it, I'll just grab a table inside, study the pictures and wait for the bomber to show up.

The hardest part will be convincing Burke that I haven't lost my mind. I've toyed with the idea of simply telling him that we're in my dream, but I'm not sure that'd make him any more cooperative.

So, I'm back to my gut, my instincts, and hoping that's enough for my partner of three years.

Eve slides the negatives into an envelope and hands them to an assistant, with the request. "Can I bum a ride back to the warehouse with you? Silas has identified some of the bomb fragments."

I have to pick up my wheels anyway, so I nod.

We drop her off at the warehouse, and with everything inside me, I want to suggest a get-together, later, at my place, something involving my shower.

But I'll wait until I wake up. Until it's real, despite the magic of this dream that allows me to smell the scent of her in Burke's car when I climb back in.

In this time, this dream, she's not mine yet, and somehow that thought puts a hand to my heart. Me, trying to be the guy I should have been.

Besides, I have more important intentions.

Dream or not, I have twelve hours before another bomb hits my city. And I plan on being there to stop it.

CHAPTER 10

"Stone really thinks there's going to be another bombing?" Silas stood at one of the long tables in the makeshift lab room, sorting bomb debris through a screen. A spotlight shone down on the fragments, the rest of the room under low light to accentuate the features. In one screen, he'd collected the shards of what looked like aluminum from the coffee thermos that held the bomb. In the second, he'd gathered the warped steel edges of a water pipe, the container that housed the low-level explosive materials, which were currently under the gas chromatograph to trace the chemical composition.

"Mmmhmm," Eve said, picking up a fragment of the pipe. Jagged edges, coated with dark residue. She took a swab of it. "He says it's a gut feeling."

Silas looked up at her, raised an eyebrow.

"I know," Eve said. "But he's…well, not what I expected. He's…earnest. And not the dark and mysterious renegade my father—and everyone else—makes him out to be. Part of me wants to believe him."

"I don't want to know what that part is," Silas said, and gave her a gimlet look. "Just watch yourself. I've heard stories."

She dropped the swab into a container and labeled it for processing. "What kind of stories?"

"Just that Rembrandt Stone is not above breaking a few rules to get answers."

If I give them answers, then maybe they can stop hoping and start figuring out how to live with the wreckage of their lives.

Rem's words, spoken as he stared into the dark amber of his beer, clung to her. A desperation, perhaps, in his tone that kneaded her own scar tissue. "Maybe sometimes you need to break a few—"

"No, Eve." Silas looked up. "That's the difference between criminal investigation and what we do. They're all about hunches and interrogations and piecing what-ifs together. We look at the facts, the evidence and find the truth. It's science, not instincts."

Silas held her gaze, and she couldn't escape the sense that it had irked him, her going out for lunch with Rembrandt. *And* Burke.

"Well, if I were to guess, given the blast wave pattern and the rate of deflagration, I think we're going to find a mix of ammonium nitrate and fuel oil in this residue."

"And maybe antimony." He held up what looked like a burned Dcell battery. "I think we have the igniter." He set the battery into the basket.

"It's not a unique chemical signature, given the pattern of the recent Oklahoma and Centennial Olympic Park bombings."

"He's a copycat at best because he used a digital alarm clock timer as the detonator." He picked up a burned mass of plastic, the wires charred.

"Which gave the bomber a twenty-four-hour window, once he set the time and attached the leads," she said, making a mental note to tell Rembrandt.

"What bombers fail to understand is that bombs do not destroy themselves in the blast. Up to ninety-five percent of the casing survives the explosion," Silas picked up a six-inch piece of mangled pipe. "What we have here is a simple pipe bomb, packed with ANFO, with a clock timer, a model rocket igniter, and activated by a battery."

Which killed seven people, including a toddler. The pretzel from the pub had turned to sludge in her stomach. She pulled off her gloves and tossed them into a nearby hazardous waste canister. "We won't know for sure if your *guess* is correct until we get the results of the chromatograph test."

Silas followed her out of the lab room into the main area where the techs were still cataloging the debris. Dim light hovered over the expanse, the cavernous room raising gooseflesh. The body of evidence felt a little like looking for the right sprig of hay in a field of mowed grass. Still, the more evidence they collected, the more information they could develop in the lab. Standing at the crime scene, amidst broken and blown-out windows, shattered furniture, the rubble of coffee machines, and even personal effects, she'd had to make some split decisions. Think like a bomber. *How would I build a bomb?*

The device would have to be undetected—hidden, perhaps under a table, in a bag, or even…and that led her to the coffee thermoses and a conversation with the arson examiner, who concurred with her theory. No, her *guess.*

Okay, fine, she'd call it a hunch. Still, Silas was right. Rules and order kept her from making crazy assumptions and veering away from the truth.

But just being around Rembrandt had made her already break some fundamentals. Like taking three hours to develop film of a crowd, in hopes of finding an unknown face at a future crime scene…yeah, he sounded crazy, and she'd drunk the Kool-Aid.

Eve walked from table to table, where the evidence technicians had not only bagged and labeled everything. Shoes, a backpack, and even the charred remnants of a coffee bean burlap sack, sketching out each item's found location on a grid of the scene.

She read the label on the burlap. *Green Earth* coffee, out of Brazil. On the table next to it lay a coffee cup, bagged, slightly crushed.

"Where was this found?" Item number forty-four—she found its number on the map. Silas came up to look over her shoulder.

"It looks like it was picked up on the sidewalk across the street. Maybe from a patron who'd just ordered their coffee and was headed to the bus stop?"

"It was on the side street, away from the shop. The bus stop is further up the street, on the opposite side."

"And there's nothing else there but the backside of the grocery store," Silas said.

"So, he was standing outside, watching?" Eve heard Rembrandt's words pinging inside her. "He thinks the bomber is trying to make a point. The early time suggests he wasn't as interested in massive casualties as he was in making a point."

"Which means he wanted to make sure it went off."

"Let's see if we can pull DNA off this. Could be nothing, but if whoever the cup belongs to was in the store, he or she might have seen something. We may have a survivor here who we missed." She handed him the baggie. "Tomorrow. Go home, Silas. It's been a long day and it's late."

"You first." Silas glanced at his watch. "Pizza?"

She scrubbed her hands down her face. "I just want to climb into my bathtub and see if I can put myself back together."

"You don't have running water," Silas said.

"Thanks for that." She followed him to the door, grabbing her satchel from the rack. "Samson promised he'd turn the water on."

Silas pushed open the door, out into the night. Overhead, stars spilled across a dark and desolate sky, pinpricks of hope, the moon an eye upon the city. She followed the puddles of street lamps out to her Escort. Silas stood at her door and hung a hand on it as she opened it.

"You sure you don't want pizza?"

He stood there, his blond hair swept back and tucked behind his ears, hazel eyes imperative.

"I gotta tell you something." He shifted, blew out a breath and adjusted his shoulder strap on his backpack. "I don't think you should be hanging out with Stone."

"I'm picking that up. Calm down, it was just lunch—"

"He didn't reveal all his secrets in that memoir of his."

She slowly rose from her seat. "I'm listening."

Silas stepped back from her door, and she closed it, then leaned against it, arms folded.

"Listen, I'm not trying to get him into trouble. It's just—"

"Tell me."

He ran his hand across his jaw. "Okay, so there was a case involving this missing four-year-old girl."

"We talked about it today, over lunch. She was kidnapped from Minnehaha Park."

"Yeah. Took them three days to find her—and when they did, she was dead."

"Sad—"

"Horrifying, because she'd also been raped. And when the coroner found that out, rumor is that your friend Rembrandt sort of lost it." He blew out a breath. "See, it was after they picked up the perp, and when the semen analysis came back, it was from…well, her father. And although there was nothing to tie the father to the kidnapping, he had contact with her either before or during the abduction. But the guy alibied out for the entire time, so…"

A chill had started in her core, begun to wring through her.

Silas seemed to be considering his next words, the way he stared out into the street, watching late night traffic cruise down the strip. The heat of the day had released from the sidewalks, now simmered in the air, mixing with the dirt and must of the city. A siren shot through the silence, whining in the distance.

"What happened?"

Silas met her eyes. "No one can prove it, but…well, the father was found beaten, nearly to death, outside a bar in St. Paul. One witness said they saw a Camaro parked on the street, but retracted it later."

"A Camaro?"

"Black." Silas' eyes narrowed. "Stone drives a black Camaro."

His words dropped through her like a stone. "You don't think…"

"I absolutely *do* think. Everyone knows he's a fighter—works out with his partner all the time at a local boxing ring."

She just stared at him. "He wouldn't…" she said softly.

He shrugged. "IA did some investigation, but rumor was Burke confirmed his alibi. Of course."

She made a non-committal noise. Then, "I might be on his side, just a little."

Silas raised an eyebrow. "No doubt it strikes a nerve in all of us to think about that little girl…and…" He shook his head. "But he nearly killed the guy, Eve."

"Supposedly."

"Really?"

"You don't know. And he was cleared."

Silas held up his hands. "All I'm saying is that the guy has a dark side. Don't get too close, okay?"

Huh. But she nodded.

He let her climb in her car, and stood there watching as she backed out. Waved before heading to his own car.

She pulled out, driving through the darkened streets toward Lake Street, then past Lake Calhoun, glistening under the moonlight in Technicolor with the lights of the city.

When she pulled up to her house, Samson's truck was parked out front. Moths played kamikaze with her lit porch light as she opened her door.

Inside, the kitchen light beckoned her and she found Samson sprawled under her sink, in his stocking feet and grout-splattered jeans. But along her kitchen counter, below the cupboards and along the back splash of her new stove, ice-blue tiles lined the walls, grouted with a foamy blue. And shoot, but Sams was right.

"Nice," she said, dropping her satchel on her countertop. Samson climbed out, knocking his hat sideways.

"Hey."

"Hey," she said.

"I have beer in the fridge." He climbed to his feet.

"I just need a bath. Please, please—"

"The water will be on in a jiffy. I need to finish connecting the new faucet."

She noticed it now, a stainless goose neck. "The place looks good, Sams."

He disappeared again under the sink. "Thanks. I know you had a rough day, so I wanted to finish it for you before you got home."

Sweet. She opened the fridge, grabbed a couple beers and when he slid back out, handed him one. He opened it, then hers and tapped their beers together.

They drank in silence.

"Is it okay if I crash on your sofa?"

She grinned. "Yeah. Or in the second bedroom upstairs."

"Great. Because I'm bushed." He picked up his pipe wrench, dropped it into an open toolbox, then closed it. "I'm going to put this in my truck."

She followed him to the door and walked out onto the porch as he went down the steps, then strode out to his Ford.

Sinking down onto the steps, she stared at the skyline in the distance, the purple lip of the IDS Tower, the shiny white of First Bank Place, and the glass curtain wall of the Piper Jaffray Building. A wall of clouds had moved in behind it, now starting to clutter the sky, and the scent of rain stirred in the hush of wind. Gooseflesh rose on her arms, despite the scrub of heat.

Samson returned and sat next to her. Took another drink, staring into the quiet neighborhood.

"I keep thinking about all those people today. They go in to buy coffee...and their lives are over, just like that." Eve touched the bottle to her lips. "It could have been me. I go into that place off Lake almost every day."

"Yeah. Think of their families, their spouses," Samson said quietly.

She picked at the label on the bottle. "There was a kid—two years old."

"Aw, man."

"I know. And...well, I had lunch with Inspectors Stone and Burke today. Rembrandt thinks it's just the beginning."

Samson glanced at her. "Rembrandt?"

She didn't pick up the bait, despite his smile. "What if he's right?"

"Why does he think there's gonna be more?"

"Instincts, he says."

Samson made a non-committal sound. Then, "Just do your job, sis. And let Stone do his."

She nodded. Took another sip of her beer, Rembrandt's voice in her head. *He's not getting away with this…not on my watch.*

Yeah, well not on hers, either.

CHAPTER 11

"I don't know what you're trying to accomplish, Rem. This is stupid."

Burke has been muttering that for the last two hours as we'd driven up and parked outside one, after another, coffee houses in the West Minneapolis area.

I'm drawing a complete blank and that fact has me wanting to bang my head against the steering wheel. I try to picture the file, the names, but only the shots from the first bombing—and perhaps the last—stand out. The last was so much more devastating. Three other buildings evacuated, an entire city block destroyed, and eight lives lost.

I still can't remember where either of them took place, however, and I'm not sure why. Maybe it's because I focused so hard on the victims, their faces deep wounds etched into my soul.

I do remember snippets—a German Shepherd running the length of a chain link fence, barking. An ice cream truck—strange, right? Tiny bells, ringing as if oblivious to the sirens, the flames licking the sky.

I also remember mannequins littering the destruction. We panicked when we first arrived and thought they were bodies.

But as hard as I dig, I can't place the location of either scene.

"We should have done this in daylight," I grouse. We spent three hours after dropping off Eve tracking down the off-duty employees of the Daily Grind, interviewing them about other employees. Even had a sit-down with the managers and the owner at the station.

All the interrogations I know will lead to nothing. No one has a motive, even the means to pull off a homemade pipe bomb.

So I admit to standing against the wall, arms akimbo as Burke prodded them for clues.

Through another window, I watched John Booker meet with families—husbands, wives, parents...

Melinda Jorgenson has a name now, as does her son, David.

I shouldn't have had that beer, because it's been trying to come back up for hours. We finally left—I insisted on driving, and have been trying to jog my memory since then.

It's dark, and the city is alive, lights splotching the pavement, the heat rising out of it from the day. A moon rose long ago, but a storm might be blowing in, the taste of it in the stir of the trees.

I'm tired. Bone weary, which is also weird because does that happen in a dream? The whole day has put me at odds with myself. I'm frayed and fighting a headache.

Burke's grumbling doesn't help. "Take me back to the station."

"Fine by me," I say and turn onto Minnehaha Avenue, heading east.

"I don't get it. You practically ignore valuable questioning from potential leads, and now, what, you're psychically trying to figure out where this guy—*if* this guy—is going to strike next?"

"I don't expect you to understand."

"Try and make me, pal, because I'm trying to be on your side here."

That throws a little ice on my ire. But I have nothing for him because even in a dream, the truth sounds impossible.

We drive in silence.

"Okay, what's eating you? You're like a man possessed today, and it doesn't add up. We're all a little shaken, but...is this about what happened in Booker's office?"

His question jerks me up, lands like a fist in my chest because I've *forgotten.*

My brother.

It happened so many years ago, the grief has a thick scab over it now, but twenty years ago, the news knocked me sideways, blurred the two events—the bombing and my brother's body recovery—together.

Now, it feels like an old, dried wound that I am reticent to pick at.

"A couple fisherman found a body of a kid in a lake near Waconia yesterday."

Silence, then, "And Booker thinks it's your brother?"

I nod.

He looks away, and releases a curse under his breath. Really, it's how I should be feeling, but like I said, the old wound has scabbed over. I've done my grieving, although I suppose when it comes to grief, it just keeps circling back around because a heaviness builds in my throat.

"Sorry."

"Yeah."

"And there was that kid today, at the scene."

David Jorgenson, which, for some reason, feels like a fresher wound, and the heaviness descends to my chest.

"Do your parents know?"

"I'm waiting for the DNA to come back before I talk to them, just, you know, to be sure."

"I suppose, having some closure will help," he says.

It will, and it does, but I just nod.

We pull up across the street from 5th Street Java and I stare at the stand-alone brick building. It has a green awning, the windows dark, the chalked specials on the window shrouded. Across the street, a twenty-four hour laundromat beams lights onto the pavement.

I roll down the window and turn off the car, trying to get a feel for the place.

"What are we doing, man?"

I sigh. And really, what does it matter? It's just a dream. It's not like Burke is going to wake up tomorrow and suddenly think, *hey, remember when you went off your rocker twenty-four years ago, and claimed that you were in a dream and predicted a bombing?*

So I turn to him. He's hidden in the darkness, just his eyes, white and confused on me as I shrug.

"I'm having a dream. A very vivid one where I'm reliving my— our—first cold case. It's three bombings. One today, one tomorrow and one the next day. And I'm trying to stop them."

He is silent, just blinking at me. Then, *"What?"*

"I know, but—listen, it's not the first time I've had this dream, although usually it stops right around the time of the first bombing, when Melinda Jorgenson goes into the coffee shop. I don't know why I'm not waking up but, as long as I'm here, I have to try and stop—"

"Are you high?"

His question knocks me back. "What? No, of course not—"

"Then, what are you talking about? This is not a dream, man. This is real." Burke's voice get intense. "Get out. I'm driving." The door opens and the dome light flickers on. I can see his face now, and he's serious, his eyes wide, shaking his head.

"Burke—"

"Shut up." He gets out and I'm not sure what to do because, well, although I expected disbelief, the anger in his voice has rocked me.

He opens my driver's door and as I turn, he hauls me bodily out of the car.

I go without resisting because I don't want to make a scene, but I give him a hard shove as soon as I hit my feet. "Step back."

Burke puts his hands up, a decoy a split second before he slams me into the car. His face is in mine and he's eying me as if he doesn't know me.

And now I'm mad, too. "I'm telling the truth. This is twenty-four years ago for me. The bomber goes uncaught, and we spend the next two decades looking at twenty faces who beg us for justice. And it's eating me alive, Burke."

I walk away from the car, then round on him. "I wake up in the middle of the night, sweating, and Eve—she tries, I know—to tell me to let it go, but I can't, right? And I know I've got everything going right for me—Ashley, and Eve and—geez, we're still friends, sort of, but—it's still there, you know? The regret. The fact that I failed so many people. And now, suddenly I'm here, dreaming, and it's not like the other times and I think, maybe I can fix it this time. And yeah, when I wake up it'll still be messed up, but at least—at least I'll know I *tried*. And maybe I won't see Melinda Jorgensen's face haunting me, carrying little David into the coffee shop."

Burke has backed away, staring at me like I'm speaking Russian. And he's shaking his head.

111

"I can't remember, though. Where the second—or third— bombings took place. You'd think I'd remember the exact location, but it's escaping me. Sort of like the lyrics to a song I *know* I should know, but can't quite put my finger on. So, I've been driving around, hoping something jogs my memory."

He frowns, a tiny smile playing on his lips. And for a second, I think, yeah, it's sadly funny. But Burke is on my team, backing me up, my partner.

He starts to laugh, shaking his head, grinning. "Geez, Rem. Seriously, you had me going there."

Huh. I lick my lips, my mouth oddly dry as he slaps one of his big maws on my shoulder. "You and Eve? Right. Yeah, dude, you *are* dreaming."

I just gape at him because, "What's so crazy about that? We're *married*. We have a kid."

"Eve Mulligan ain't ever gonna marry you." He laughs. "Saying she's out of your league is like saying Fran Tarkenton was a sorta okay quarterback."

I know that, but it hurts a little to see Burke so convinced.

"I'll have you know that Eve thinks…she's a fan. We're good together."

Burke comes close now, is staring into my eyes, searching. "I don't know why you're pranking me, but…good one. You sounded as serious as a heart attack."

"I *am* serious."

"Mmmhmm. Okay, it's time to call it a night."

He pushes past me and climbs into the driver's seat.

"Hey."

"What did I just tell you? I'm driving. Get in if you want a ride."

I stifle a word and head around to the passenger side. "I have three more shops on my list."

"Forget it. I'm taking you home."

I shake my head, but he puts the car into drive. "If it's a dream, you can wake up tomorrow and start over. I know, maybe you can take a look at the file and figure out where the shops were, save us some time, huh?"

He's smirking, mocking me, but the words, the idea slips into my head.

I'll do exactly that. When I wake up, I'll go over the case. Then when night hits, I'll take another sleeping pill, or whatever knocked me into this loop and find myself back in time, *starting over*.

And I'll do things right with Eve, too. I won't knock coffee on her, but I'll figure out something witty to say. This time I'll score a date, without Burke, and figure out a way to fast-track our romance.

Not spend ten years figuring out that I can't live without her. Because Burke is right, she is way out of my league, and doesn't deserve what I put her through.

So I settle back in my seat as Burke turns us around, down to Chicago Avenue, then south to Lake, and west to Holmes. He pulls up in front of the brownstone.

It takes me a second. Because I don't yet live on Washburn in our updated craftsman.

He hands me my key off my ring. "I'll pick you up in the morning."

I pile out and stand there as he leaves me. And now I get it.

He thinks I've lost it, or maybe yes, high, although it's been at least thirty years since my last joint. So he's left me on the curb to sleep off the crazy.

Hmm.

I head inside the brownstone and up the stairs to the third floor. My key fits into the lock as if it knows the way and suddenly, I'm inside my old digs. Shadows fall through the front window blinds and stripe the oak floor. I'm not a messy person—never have been, but admittedly, Eve has trained me, so I'm not surprised to see a T-shirt crumpled on the sofa where I last used it as a pillow. And on the floor of my room, a pair of socks.

The kitchen is as I left it, twenty-two years ago, with last night's containers in the trash. Chou's take out—how I loved their Kung Pao Chicken. I walk over and open the fridge. Mostly empty save for a half of a six pack of Coke, a corked bottle of Cabernet, and a piece of blueberry pie from Betty's Bodacious Bakery down the street.

My stomach roars and I take out the foam container, pour myself a half glass of the wine and let myself sink into the tangy sweetness of Betty's fantastic pie, well missed.

I lick out the container, and love every minute of it. Taking my wine out to the front room, I stare down at the street.

Rain has started to fall, a patter on the windows, hazing the street lamps, a rhythmic beat that presses the fatigue further into my bones.

Yeah, maybe it's time to sleep. To wake up, roll over and pull Eve into my arms, press my lips against her skin, inhale. Today she was beautiful and young and everything I remembered about the woman I love and I'm suddenly hungry for her.

If I had my car, I might even drive by that old bungalow on Webster. Because a guy can be a stalker in a dream and not call it creepy.

I finish the wine, set the glass in the sink, and head to my bedroom, unbuttoning my shirt, pulling off my dress pants. I stand in front of the mirror a second.

Flex.

Oh, I miss this body.

I climb into bed, thunder rolling over me, a slash of light from the storm breaking the dark veneer of the room. But I close my eyes.

Sink into my pillow. Because it's been a good, *very good* dream. A reminder of the way my world was with Eve before the cracks appeared.

I swear I'm only out for moments, when I hear the banging.

It beats with the hammer in my head.

"Rem!"

I know the voice, and in the cling of slumber I wonder what Burke is doing here, at my house at this ungodly hour. But even as I roll over, flinging an arm over my eyes, I can see the dent of light, the graying of morning.

I pat the bed. Eve is up and has been for a while because the sheets are cold from her absence.

"Rem!" He bangs on the door three more times. I sit up—which turns out to be a bad move because my entire brain shifts in my head like sloshing water.

"Coming!"

I groan because my head really hurts. I scrub a hand down my face, then open my eyes.

Everything inside me goes cold.

I'm not in my bedroom, the sun cascading through a stained-glass transom at the head of my bed. Eve is not standing at the doorway, yelling at Burke to let me sleep in, and Ashley is not pushing past her to bounce in, pounce on me, her hands finding my face for a good morning smooch.

I stumble across the bedroom floor, then to the front door of the apartment and pull it open.

It's just Burke, standing there in a puddle of early morning light, sliding in across my tiny apartment living room. Young, with hair, that stupid soul patch, and he looks a little like he's going to hit me, something gnarled and dark in his expression.

"What—what are you doing here?"

"How did you know?"

"Know what—?"

He strides past me then whirls around. "Get ready. We gotta roll."

I press my palm to my temple, head still feeling thick as tar. C'mon, I had a half a glass of wine, for Pete's sake.

And that was yesterday, in my dream.

Except...

The tan carpet is soft against my bare feet, my young man's body awake for the morning ... I'm still here.

In 1997.

"Know what?" I say for the second time.

"A second bombing. It hit the coffee shop on Lyndale and 35th. Five people dead so far. *How did you know?*"

I'm shaking as I go into the bathroom, turn on the water, splash it on my face. Because that's what people do when they're losing it. When they can't believe the reality thrown at them. When they want, desperately, to wake up.

When they realize that, I don't know how, but ... *this is not a dream.*

CHAPTER 12

I rode by Mickey's bike the first time in my half-frantic, growing panic, my legs churning, my throat stripped from screaming his name.

Only on my second pass up the road did I spot a flash of red. Half-hidden in the grasses, a clump of daisies jutting through the spokes as if in silent sympathy, the bike lay crushed, violated.

Beaten.

It lay in the weeds, tossed haphazardly aside as if a nuisance. A red Mini Viper, with platinum racing stripes on the fender, a foam cushion across the front bar, padded handlebars and dirt-bike wheels. Mickey got it for his eighth birthday only two weeks before he disappeared.

The front tire rim sagged, as if it had hit a boulder, dumping the rider over the handlebars. Dimples marked the paint, and a scrub across the red revealing the silver frame told the story of a struggle against the dirt road.

As if Mickey had scrabbled to his feet, tried to right the bike.

And was taken mid-action.

There's a hiccup in time when tragedy occurs, a moment before it becomes personal, the information still clinical, still objective before it settles into a person's brain, trickles into their bones, poisons their blood. It's in this moment the instinct of disbelief kicks in, an invisible hand that snakes out to stiff arm the truth.

To protect.

To prepare the body for the onslaught of truth.

I felt it as I stared at Mickey's bike, my breath catching.

I know it now as Burke pulls up to the morning's carnage in my Camaro—he's driving—and it's a good thing because I could barely think enough to put on pants, my soiled dress shirt, grab a suit coat.

Frankly, I only move now because Burke is out of the car and striding ahead, toward Booker, who watches the scene with folded arms.

Burke hasn't spoken to me since we left my apartment, his question still ringing in my head. *How did you know?*

I had no answer for him as I walked out of the bathroom, because my only explanation feels pitiful and even irreverent. I *dreamed* it?

This can't possibly be a dream.

The pungent odor of burned flesh hazes the air, turning my gut. The smoke bites my eyes, and sirens rend the air. The drizzle of spray coats my neck, and behind the raucousness, I can hear Minneapolis's finest shouting as they work to douse the fire.

It's a house turned coffee shop. Why didn't I remember that? I had all the pieces—the barking dog—not a German shepherd, but a Doberman running the length of the yard across the street, imprisoned behind chain link. And, down the street, an ice cream truck, parked in a driveway. Maybe I imagined the bells ringing.

The house is an old Victorian-turned unique venue. Now, it's simply a house fire, flames consuming the upstairs windows, the porch collapsing, the front windows blown out. Glass glints orange against the flames.

Smoke blots out the skyline, just the finest edge of sunlight through the black.

I'm without words, caught in the catastrophe, one thought like a fist in my still hammering head. *I could have stopped this.*

Should have stopped this. Right?

I join Burke, the questions tangled in the chaos of my brain.

"Four dead, one on the way to HCMC," Booker says without preamble. Hennepin County Medical Center. Two more ambulances are coming, but the only victims remaining are covered in tarps.

Burke glances at me. "This place was on the list."

I frown, because the last thing I want John Booker to know is, well, *everything*.

Booker looks at me anyway, frowning. "What list?" He wears a stony, all business expression.

"A list of coffee shops," I interject before Burke can throw me under the bus. "Possible other targets."

Booker raises an eyebrow. Frowns.

That's the moment my gaze falls on his wrist. On his watch. The watch *I'm* currently wearing. It's a lightning bolt, right through me. The *watch*.

The one I'm also wearing. I look at it.

It's still ticking.

"Rem thought it was going to happen again," Burke says, the Judas. "And he was right."

Booker's frowning at me and I parlay the words into action. "The bomber could be in the crowd, right now, just like last time. We should be looking for a familiar face."

For the first time, something reasonable appears on Burke's expression and he doesn't look like he'd like to pin me to the wall for some questioning. Instead he heads back to the car, and it takes me a second to realize he's probably going to consult the pictures Eve gave us yesterday.

Booker is still staring at me, however. "Possible other targets? Why?"

"Bombers usually have reasons for their targets. Why a coffee shop? Why *this* coffee shop? There has to be a connection between these two." Or three, I think, but I'm keeping that to myself for now.

Booker draws in a breath, then nods. But his gaze lingers on me, as if searching for something. He finally turns away. "Find that reason. Now."

I hear ticking in my head as I follow Burke to the car. He's retrieved the pictures now and has them spread out on the hood of the car.

Beyond him, Eve has arrived, her CSI side-kick Silas in tow. She looks tired, her kinky hair pulled back, and she wears no make-up as if she, too, got yanked out of bed.

She's probably reeling, trying to find her footing, like me.

"We should interview people, see if anyone saw anything," Burke says as I join him. He glances up at the crowd, as if searching.

Onlookers have assembled, just a handful of them this early in the morning, and God help me, I suddenly don't remember *anything*. Did we interview anyone before? Did we track down the employees, cross-reference any of them with the other store? Did we discover commonalities?

Did we suspect that this was all connected? It's a strange deja vu because I know I've been here before, but my memory is liquid.

"You see anyone watching?" Burke says, his voice cut low.

I glance at the pictures, casually, then scan the growing crowd. This area of town is rife with young professionals, many on bicycles, a few standing at the bus station. Neighbors congregate on porches, at the doors of their homes. A few cars have drivers standing with their doors open.

I'm going to need help.

I find Eve, still struck by the scene, judging by the look on her pale face.

"We need crowd pictures. Lots of them."

She turns, her eyes wide. My tone is dark, brusque, but this is no longer a what-if.

"Now."

She frowns, and I know that face. The one I get when I've pushed her, when she's debating a retort. But we don't have time for feelings, not when the suspect could be vanishing into the crowd.

I feel the passionate, darkly focused Rembrandt I've left behind working his way to the surface.

Good. Frankly, I need him.

"Right." She has her camera and she starts snapping shots, along with Silas.

I return to Burke. He's interviewed a couple spectators, written down names, and now he's leaning against the car, staring at the crowd, then back at the pictures, comparing.

"Anything?"

He glares at me, his eyes dark.

"Tell me, right now, that you don't know anything about this," he says, low and nearly under his breath. But his tone contains enough of an edge that it leaves a mark.

"Of course not. I told you, it was—*is*—a hunch."

He nods then and holds up a picture to the crowd assembled behind the fire trucks.

Why *this* coffee shop? My question to Booker needles me. It's not a chain store, rather an artsy hole-in-the wall. I remember donuts being served from the back patio during an art show I attended shortly after I moved to the neighborhood. Donuts and organic coffee.

The explosion has littered said coffee—beans and grounds—along with glass and debris onto the street. A piece of burlap is soaked and tattered on the pavement. My gaze lands on it, and something about the logo—four leaves, four beans—nudges me.

I'm not sure why I pick it up, but a memory sloshes through my brain.

It's cut off by the sight of a woman advancing on the scene. She's young, dark hair and with a jolt, I remember her. Only, not from the past, but from my present. My *real* life.

Mariana Vega, real estate investor and current mayor of St. Louis Park, my district. She's younger, of course, her hair long and in tangles, but she still possesses the take-no-prisoners approach she lives by in city council meetings.

The kind of stance that can deny a guy a building permit—appeal pending—for a second story on his garage, an addition that would make the perfect office. Maybe a place where a writer's words wouldn't get tangled, stuck—

"She looks upset," Burke says.

She's yelling at Booker, gesturing to the shop. Her face is streaked with tears, however, and she's almost sympathetic.

"She's the owner."

I'm not sure how I know that, but it feels like the right answer. And, despite our history and my clear memory of her cold-hearted verdict against my muse, I feel a twinge at her distress.

Although, maybe the insurance is her seed money for her massive empire. A random and unlikely motive, but I tuck that information away, and return to the pictures spread out on the Camaro.

"Hey," Burke says quietly. His tone makes me look up. He's staring past me, toward Eve, but beyond. "See the guy in the neon green shirt?"

I glance at the man. Maybe in his late twenties, he's well over six feet, with inky black hair and a dark gaze that is seared on Mariana.

"Does he look like this guy?" Burke points to a man in a shot at yesterday's scene. The man in the picture is standing across the street from the bombing, holding a coffee cup.

Could be. Dark hair, and although he's wearing a baseball cap in the picture, the face seems similar.

Everything inside me ignites. *Please.*

"Close enough," I growl and in a breath I'm sprinting.

I shoot past Eve even as I hear Burke give a shout. But I'm not slowing down.

I want him. Just to question, to put the pieces together, but my gut is screaming—*yes.*

Maybe this, right here, is why I'm here. I still don't know how, but maybe, cosmically, there is a God out there who follows my nightmares, the cold clench the past has on my life.

And maybe He's dishing out do-overs.

Neon has spotted me and a spark of panic flashes across his unshaven face a second before he turns and *runs.*

See? *Instincts.*

The bugger is fast, has longer legs and is in shape.

But so am I. This younger me has chops and I'm churning up the sidewalk like a man on fire. "Stop!" I yell because I'm supposed to, right? But there's not gonna be a response.

Neon doesn't even glance over his shoulder as he motors down the sidewalk.

He passes Aldrich, Bryant, and cuts south on Colfax.

I motion to Burke, hopefully behind me, to keep going and I follow Neon between two houses, across an alley, and over to Dupont.

He crosses the median, to the honking of a car, and thinks he's going to lose me in the cemetery.

Hardly. I ran track in high school. And I have my young lungs back.

Burke's yelling behind me, but I'm not losing this guy. He's agile and fast, as if used to running. That's my brain already applying judgment, I know, but it fuels me as my lungs burn.

Lakewood Cemetery is 250 acres of mausoleums and headstones cluttered with trees and footpaths.

I know this place.

I gesture Burke to angle down the footpath while I veer right to cut off Neon. He heads across open ground, past an alley of headstones and markers, trampling over them with impunity.

Spotting Burke, he cuts right. Well, Burke would scare me, too, sprinting right at him like a defensive end.

But Neon is *my* prey and when he trips over a marker, I leap.

He's bigger, more solid, than I anticipate and shrugs me off even as we slam into the grass. I'm rolling and on my feet before he can find his. I take him down with a fist to the jaw.

My hand explodes, but Neon takes the hit like he's expecting it. He shakes it off and lets out a curse.

"Get down!" I yell, but he's not having it. Incredibly, he lunges at me.

That's all I need to unleash everything inside me. The queasy, irritating deja vu that has me stuck in the past. The horror of the desecration of so many lives and frankly, even the sweat pouring down my back and the burn in my fist.

I'm here because of him.

He's tackled me, but I trap his legs, pull his head down into my shoulder and slam my fist into his ear. He struggles, so I hit him again, and when he pushes away from me, I flip on him, my knee in his gut and crunch my fist into his face.

It's all blurring now—the shouting, the heat rolling off me, the cursing of the man fighting back.

He lands a couple blows in my ribs, but I'm impervious. Then Burke pulls me off, shoves me away "Step back, Rem!"

He grabs Neon in an arm bar, flipping him onto his stomach. "You—stop moving. Stay down!"

Neon stops struggling and I sink to the grass, breathing hard.

Burke shoots me a look. "What's wrong with you?"

Me? I stare at him. "What—he was in the crowd!"

"Maybe," Burke says, his hand still on Neon's back. Now, he leans in close to the man. "Talk. Why'd you run?"

Neon swallows, glares at me, shakes his head. There's a confusion on his face that doesn't make sense, and there's nothing clicking in, no memory that might clear this up.

"Let him go!"

The voice travels across the green, sharp and resonant, authority in the tone. Booker?

What is Booker doing here? He strides up, a little out of breath. And behind him—Mariana? She's parked her car on the street and is running across the grass in her bare feet.

125

"Let him go!" She echoes Booker's words and I get a sick feeling.

Burke has risen, backing off Neon who rolls over, spit in his eyes. And by the way Booker glares at me, I know I'm going to have some explaining to do. I'm still sitting on the grass, however, catching my breath.

"This is Ramses Vega—Mariana's son," Booker says and extends a hand to the man. "You okay?"

Ramses looks at me as if he'd like to have another go at me, and barring Booker, (and maybe Burke) he would.

Let's go, buddy, I say with my eyes as I climb to my feet. My shirt is torn, grass stains my suit pants. I don't even try to brush them off. This is why I stopped wearing dress clothes to work.

"I have my reasons, boss," I say to Booker and he considers me for a moment even as Mariana runs up and throws her arms around Ramses. He embraces her, dark eyes glued on me.

"What is your problem?" Mariana shrieks, and there go my chances of getting that garage addition.

"He was at yesterday's bombing," I say quietly.

Ramses presses his thumb to the corner of his mouth, and he's sporting a doozy of a goose-egg under his eye. I'm sure I have my own war wounds, but you don't see me whining.

"And today's."

Only now do I realize that Mariana has turned to him and is translating for him.

No wonder he looked so confused.

He responds in Portuguese, a deduction I make when it pings in my brain that Mariana is Brazilian.

"He *was* there yesterday," she says, her voice a little shaky. "He was going to class. He attends English class at the Calvary Baptist

Building, at the immigrant school there. The coffee shop is a block away from the school."

My memory can't confirm that, but it doesn't matter because Booker is apologizing to Mariana, taking her hand, wearing apology on his face.

Listen, don't go that easy on her, I want to say, but Booker is a nicer guy than me.

Ramses and his mother head back to the car as Booker rounds on me. "Another instinct?"

"He was at both places," I say. "C'mon, boss."

Booker's looking at me again as if trying to see through me. "You can do better than this," he says finally and turns, heading back to the scene.

Burke however, lifts a shoulder, gives a half-grin. "He nearly took you."

I shake my head, not ready to let this go. Because it's a little weird to me that that Mariana ran an entire election campaign, her face plastered on signs and leaflets around my neighborhood for the better part of a year and not once did I see—or hear mention of—her immigrant son.

As if he simply didn't exist.

That question is a burr under my skin all the way back to the scene. The crowd is dispersing, the fire trucks packing up, the fire fighters walking through the now charred, smoking house.

I spot Eve taping off the scene, and I want to go over to her, but maybe I don't have time to smooth things over.

Because—I feel it in my gut, along with the realization that I'm in way over my head—this is real.

And I'm running out of time.

CHAPTER 13

This is not my reality. How can it be? That thought pulses with every heartbeat, slowly turning into a sledgehammer in my head.

I need coffee, and suggested it on the drive to the precinct, but Burke looked at me as if I'd declared I wanted to stroll naked down Nicollet Mall.

I'm currently drinking the sludge out of the green coffee pot on the side table. I'm effectively holding up the wall, my head leaned back, feeling like something that slept in an alley off Hennepin Avenue.

Booker has procured another whiteboard. Five new faces, two female employees, one male employee, a mechanic from the local body shop, and a Vietnamese woman who ran the Vo's takeout (I know her son—he runs the place now and it serves excellent Goi Cuon). The music minister at the Presbyterian church on the corner is fighting for his life at HCMC ICU.

The victims were quickly identified by Mariana, a job I don't envy.

I'm still niggling on the fact that Ramses has so totally fallen off the grid, in my world.

My world. That's how I'm thinking, as if I'm a visitor here, the precinct not where I spent twenty meaningful years, Burke some cousin of the real Andrew, back in, well, my world.

And Eve. Eve is the younger, easier-going version of the woman I am really starting to miss. Not that I don't like this Eve, but I need the Eve who can knock me back into play, unravel the knots in my brain.

I need answers, and not just about the second bombing, but… *all* the answers.

It's an action from Booker that gives me a lead. He is standing at the front of the room, listing the what-we-knows and results of yesterday's bombing (pretty much what Eve suggested, a homemade bomb, although I know all that already) when I see him glance at the back. To the clock on the wall.

It's a quick, almost nonchalant, *practiced* glance and it occurs to me…why isn't he looking at his watch?

The watch I'm wearing, incidentally, which is still working, purring along as if it never had a glitch.

"I gotta run an errand," I say to Burke. Although Booker has assigned us lead investigators on yesterday's bombing, he's clearly helming today's update. We'll spend the morning interviewing employees and creating files on the deceased.

Burke looks at me, frowns. "Another *hunch?*"

Touchy. "No." I say, but yeah, that conversation is looming. I have to give him some reason for my soon-to-commence search for the location of bombing number three, a fact that still eludes me.

Not that I would remember well. Shortly after arriving at the third bombing scene, I got a call from dispatch and spent the rest of the day pacing the HCMC waiting area as my mother fought for her life.

That memory I remember with brutal clarity.

I guess a stroke is a natural reaction to hearing the long-dreaded news about your missing son, especially when one suffers from high blood pressure.

But if I'd been there that morning as my father headed out to the barn with the sunrise, when the sheriff showed up with the news, maybe the blow would have been softer.

Maybe even better if I had delivered it.

I make a mental note to check in with Booker about the DNA results and head outside into the sunshine, the bright, blue-skied day a betrayal to this morning's devastation.

My Camaro is parked in the shade and I slide in, crank down the windows and hang my elbow out as I cruise toward Uptown. I turn on KQRS and find an oldie playing ... well, maybe not that old anymore.

Styx, "Come Sail Away."

I wish.

I turn off Lake to Hennepin and park in front of the Uptown theater. I cut across the road, past the McDonald's and down the alley to the American Vintage Watch Repair, looking for a younger version of my Asian friend.

Same dim hallway, but at the end I find a small room advertising a coin-operated tanning bed. No sign of the workshop, the wooden bench, the giant magnifying glass, or the not-so-helpful watchmaker.

I walk back into the sunlight, a crazy thought slivering into my brain.

Stillwater.

Please.

Even the little ditty about Jack and Diane refuses to lighten my mood as I drive south. I pull into the parking lot near the river, two blocks from the house, in front of a used bookstore, someday to be a coffee shop, and head down to the Tudor. The white stucco is freshly painted and the chimney is not yet in disrepair. The door is a pale pine, not yet stained, and a cheery geranium sits in the pot by the door. The hosta hasn't matured, the Japanese maple a shadow of its future self.

I don't know why, but I feel like a kid at Halloween, ready to shout trick or treat—and mostly *trick*—as I press the creepy doorbell.

Is it crazy to think this old guy might remember me? He's never seen me before, and it's a much younger version who opens the door, frowning at me.

The next twenty years will be hard on him. Not as bone thin, he looks well-fed, less brittle, and certainly a gentler version of himself despite the gray hair, cut military short.

Life hasn't yet beaten him. His blue eyes widen when I say, "I need your help."

I know. It's a pretty desperate move, but what would you do if you were wrestling with the idea that this trip through *time* could be real?

"That so," he says.

I hold out my hand. "Inspector Rembrandt Stone. I'm working a couple bombings in Minneapolis—"

"I saw that on the news." He shakes his head.

"Who is it, Art?" A voice emerges from behind him and a woman appears. Her long brown hair is pulled back, glasses atop her head and she's wearing a white halter top, a pair of jeans, and is barefoot. She pushes past her husband. "Sheila Fox. How can we help you, Detective?"

So, she must have heard something. She has a firm handshake despite the delicate bones of her hand, and the look of a professor as she pulls me over the threshold.

The home is immaculate, and bright. It possesses the wide crown moldings and arched doorways of a classic 1930s Tudor, narrow planked pine wood flooring, a comfortable family room with leather overstuffed chairs and heavy brocade draperies, a piano in the corner, and a neat, but cluttered knee wall bookcase. The kind of house in which I would not have had to look hard to find my muse. It smells of pipe smoke, maybe a pot roast in the kitchen.

Art is not thrilled I'm standing in his entry way, but he closes the door behind me. "We don't have anything to do with the bombings," he says, "so I'm not sure how we can help you."

"Lemonade?" Sheila asks.

I could use something stiffer, maybe, but I nod and she heads to the kitchen.

"I suppose I have to invite you in now," Art says.

"I hear you can fix vintage pieces."

I point to my watch and study his expression. He glances at it and lets a tiny frown dip down over one eye, then nods and heads down the hall. "This way."

I follow him to a study, or perhaps a workshop because it contains a desk, a magnifying glass, and the familiar surgical instruments I remember from Vintage American.

"What's wrong with it?" he asks, and I unbuckle the watch from my wrist.

"Um ... well, actually, nothing right now." I hand him the watch. "But it wasn't working back in…well, actually, that's why I'm here. See…I think I'm," and here goes nothing, "from the future."

I say it without my voice shaking, incidentally, which I think deserves props.

He just looks at me. A grandfather clock ticks somewhere in the room, or down the hall. Or in my head.

"Let me see the watch."

I hand it over. He studies it, then turns it over. Runs his thumb over the words inscribed.

"Be Stalwart."

"I inherited it."

"Mmmhmm." He takes it over to his desk, sets it down. "From whom?"

Oh. "My...well, my boss, Chief of Police, John Booker."

He nods again and the fact he hasn't jumped on my words, *I think I'm from the future* has a crackle buzzing under my skin.

He picks up what looks like the same stethoscope he used before, or in the future (see how confusing this is?) and presses it to the watch, listening, like it might have a heartbeat.

Of course it does.

"It didn't work when I first got it and then..." *I brought it to you.* Yes, I nearly say that, but I yank the words back because then I'd *really* sound nuts.

Besides, it has occurred to me, slowly, that something has happened to his wife over the past twenty-plus years, and I don't want to be trapped into having to expound how we know each other. He might start asking questions.

I might start having to lie.

But I feel for him. If I lost Eve I'd end up stripped of life, gaunt, hollowed out. So I finish with, "...suddenly, yesterday, it started working."

"How?" He puts down the stethoscope.

"I was..." I'm searching my brain to catalog the exact events. "In my study. And I was looking over my old cold cases—one of these being the bombing from yesterday, and today..." *And tomorrow.* I debate that and skip over it. "And suddenly the watch started working."

"You wound it, right?"

I frown. Then. "Yes."

"Then, of course, it started working."

"What do you mean, *of course it started working*? It wasn't working before. At all. Then…it just started ticking."

He lifts a shoulder. "That's how it's supposed to work. It's a timepiece. It ticks off time." He hands the watch back to me. "It looks like it's working exactly how it's intended."

I stare at him. Because, well, you know, *that's what he said before.* Or *will* say.

Oh brother.

"What do you mean?"

"I think you know what I mean," he says and stands up.

I have no idea what he's talking about. "It's…did you hear me? I think I…" I close my eyes, wincing even as I say it. "I think I *traveled in time.*"

Silence, and I open my eyes. He stares at me, one eyebrow raised.

I can't stop myself, the words rushing out, a catharsis. "By twenty-four years. One minute it's 2021 the next…" I shake my head. "The next I'm watching the past repeat itself. I'm watching people die, again. And today…well, I thought it was a dream at first, but…" I press my hand to my forehead because my head is pounding.

He considers me, arms crossed over his chest long enough for me to think maybe I'm losing my mind. Behind him, the sun's rays filter through the window, tiny particles dancing on the streams, and the room is turning woozy and hot.

Maybe, really, maybe this *is* a dream, the variety that involves me being hospitalized. Maybe I was hit by a car and I'm in a coma—

"*Be Stalwart*," he says quietly.

I look up at him.

"It means be dependable."

"I know what it means."

"Loyal."

"Mmmhmm."

"Faithful, devoted, unwavering—"

"*I know what it means!*"

"And?" His voice falls. "Are you?"

I blink at him. Open my mouth. Close it. "I don't know."

That's when the room starts to pitch. Sideways, my head about to explode. I reach for the wall and find instead his hand on my arm, guiding me to a chair.

I dip my head forward, cradling it in my hands.

His hand falls on my shoulder. "Cold cases, you say?"

So he was listening. I nod.

"Unanswered questions, promises unkept."

I draw in a breath. Look up at him. "Is this real?"

"Tell me. How did you find me?" Those blue eyes hold mine like a vice.

"We met before."

He gives the slightest of nods. "We *will* meet, then."

I return the nod.

"And what do I tell you?"

"That…that the watch is working."

He smiles. "Indeed."

His hand squeezes my shoulder and a moment later, Sheila comes in with the lemonade. She hands it to me. "Fresh squeezed. Nothing artificial. But it's a little tart, so be careful." Then she grins and takes Art's hand just like Eve has taken mine for the past million years.

I really miss Eve.

"Can I get back?" I whisper, taking a drink. It *is* tart, and my throat tightens, my eyes burning.

"Yes." He pauses and draws in a breath. "I think so."

A fist releases inside me.

"Can I change things?"

"How would I know?" he says quietly.

"How long am I here?"

He lifts a shoulder. "But I think you should hurry."

I finish the lemonade, and down the hallway, the grandfather clock chimes.

He takes the glass from me and nods toward the door. "Be stalwart, Inspector Stone."

CHAPTER 14

"I suppose you're going to miss a lot more breakfasts."

Eve looked up from the magnifying glass and her examination of the fabric that matched the bomber's backpack to spot her father as he came into her lab. Inspector Mulligan held his jacket by a thumb over his shoulder, his tie loosened, a haze of whiskers on his face.

"Are you just getting off, or are you starting your shift?"

He dropped the jacket on a nearby folding chair and came over, pressed a kiss to her forehead. "Just getting off and heading home now. We missed you this morning."

"We have to catch this guy." She offered him a smile, the best she could give at the moment. After eight hours dissecting the debris from today's Lyndale bombing, sorting evidence, ordering tests and sketching out a preliminary crime scene, her feet ached, her eyes burned.

"Your poor mother." He shook his head. "In her head, you're still thirteen."

"She's not the only one who thinks that." She raised an eyebrow.

"Fifteen, max," he said and winked. "Why are you the only one here?"

"Silas will be back any minute. He went downtown to drop off samples for testing, but we're fairly sure the bomber used the same ingredients as the Franklin Avenue bomb—ammonium nitrate, fuel oil, and antimony sulfide."

She pulled off her rubber gloves, touched her pinky to a black residue on a slide tray. "Taste this."

"What? No."

She laughed. "Chicken. If you did, you'd discover it tastes sweet, and a little metallic. That's antimony sulfide. It's used in fireworks. And in its pure form, is used in batteries and even bullets."

"Fireworks, huh?"

"Mmmhmm. This time, the bomb was packed into an old thermos, the kind someone might use for soup in their lunch." She pointed to the torn, curved metallic shards. "Smaller than yesterday's, although still deadly."

She walked over to the scene, sketched out on a grid on a nearby table. "After talking to the fire chief and measuring the burn and blast patterns, we think the backpack was left behind the counter, near the supply of beans."

"An employee?"

"Or at least *someone* who had access. Although, according to Burke, he and Rembrandt interviewed all the employees and they all alibied out."

"Rembrandt. As in Inspector Stone." Her father's eyebrow went up. "You're working with him?"

She grabbed a nearby stool and slid onto it. "Dad. I work in the Minneapolis Police Department. So does he. Of course I'm going to run into Inspector Stone. He's lead on the case."

He ran a hand under his chin. "And does that include eating dinner together?"

She gritted her teeth. This was why she needed to move to another state.

"I ate with Inspector Stone *and* Burke."

Her father's mouth tightened into a grim line. "You heard what happened today, at the scene, right? With Rembrandt?"

"That he ran down a possible suspect?"

She hadn't just heard about it, she'd watched as he tore past her, lean and quick and fierce, the expression on his face sending a spark through her she couldn't identify.

Not fear, really, but perhaps, well, warning.

The kind that said she might have glimpsed a layer of Rembrandt that accompanied Silas's accusation.

"He *attacked* the guy. John's thinking he might file police brutality charges."

She sighed and ran a hand behind her neck. Squeezed a muscle there. "The scene was awful, Dad. I've seen burned bodies before, but…it's a terrible way to die. It's different, you know, to be there. To see it. Again. And to know…well," She caught her bottom lip in her teeth.

"To know?"

"It's just…Stone had this hunch that it was going to happen again." She didn't want to betray him, but maybe they should all pay a bit more attention to his instincts.

Her father gave a quick frown, just a flicker. "What kind of hunch?"

"He made me print off all the pictures from the crowd yesterday and was studying them. That's why—well, *probably* that's why he went after this guy. Burke said the guy was at the bombing yesterday."

Her father's frown returned.

"And Inspector Stone just ran after him?"

She lifted a shoulder.

"Rembrandt Stone is a hot-head, who's impulsive decisions are going to get other people killed."

She opened her mouth, not sure what to say. Closed it. Then, "I blew up the pictures from today, too."

Gesturing him to follow her, she walked over to a whiteboard where she'd pinned up the pictures. Today's on one board, yesterday's on the one beside it.

Her dad studied the pictures. "You think that the bomber stayed to watch."

"Yes, I do." The voice came from behind them; a quiet, deep tenor that made her turn.

Rembrandt might have had a worse day than both of them. His cheek boasted a purpling bruise, his eyes tired, reddened. And he must have been wrestling a hand through his hair, one side of it rucked up. He dumped his jacket on her worktable and unbuttoned the sleeves of his grass-stained shirt, rolling one sleeve, then the other, up past his elbows. No tie today, and his suit pants hung low on his hips, also stained.

"Ramses was at the first scene. He said he was getting coffee, but why would a guy get coffee from a different location if his mother ran a coffee shop?" He came right up to the boards, crossed his arms over his chest.

He had nice shoulders, powerful forearms, and she sort of wished she'd seen that fight, especially after the rumors of how he'd tackled the suspect and kept him down.

Apparently the sluice of warning hadn't taken hold.

Or perhaps her own instincts simply detected a different kind of danger.

"These are the shots from today?"

She nodded. "We spent the day looking for similarities."

"Why don't you run them through a facial recognition program, see if the computer can find a match?"

She stared at him. "I've heard about that. The Bochum system, out of Germany. I think they've developed a similar program at USC. I'd love to get my hands on it."

He glanced over at her, gave a quick frown, blinking. "Yeah. Maybe someday." Then, "I'm going to need copies of these."

"I already made them."

She didn't miss the glance from her father before she walked across the room, to her makeshift desk, to grab the manila envelope.

When she returned, she caught the tail end of her father's words, low and clipped. "...her into trouble."

She should have moved to Duluth. Or maybe Anchorage. "Inspector Mulligan?" she said, and her father glanced at her without even a hint of embarrassment.

He just smiled at her. "Stop by the house tomorrow. Your mother worries." He leaned in and popped a kiss on her forehead.

Now she felt fifteen.

Rembrandt wore a strange, almost soft expression watching her father stride from the room.

Then he turned back to the boards. "He thinks I'm going to get you into trouble."

"I'm just doing my job. Which is to follow the evidence." She handed him the envelope. "And help you catch this guy."

"I appreciate it."

Rem appeared so wrung out that she quelled the strangest—and inappropriate—urge to touch his arm. Maybe suggest a beer.

Still. "You okay?"

He glanced at her. "You ever think about it?"

"About what?"

"You walk into a coffee shop, on your way to work, and order a latte, and then, *boom*. It's over. Your life, done."

She drew in a breath. "No. Or, not usually. Today, however…"

"Right?" He walked over to her table, leaned on one of the metal benches and crossed his arms. "What would you regret?"

She had followed him over, sat on the chair from where her father had retrieved his coat. "Regret?"

"You know—do over again, if you could? With what you know now."

She considered him, the way he was studying her. He had amazing eyes, deep blue, the kind a girl could fall into and never come up for air. "I don't know. Maybe I'd tell my friend, Stefanie, not to trust the cross-country coach."

His eyebrow went up. "That's who you think killed her? The girl who got run over?"

She nodded. "But it's just a—"

"Hunch." His smile stirred coals deep down inside.

No, no…she shook her head, not smiling. "A hunch only gets you so far. You need evidence to close a case."

"Fair enough," he said, his expression turning serious. "And was there any evidence?"

"It was a hit and run, so…no."

He gave a grim nod.

Silence hung between them.

"If I could go back in time, I'd tell myself not to ask Dougie Randall to the 10th Grade Sadie Hawkins dance."

He raised an eyebrow, one side of his mouth tweaking up. "Yeah?"

She ran her hands up her arms, not sure why she'd said that, but she liked the sudden spark in his eye, so, "I called him up, asked for Doug, and then rattled off an invitation to the dance. But then it got real quiet on the other line and this deep voice finally said, 'I think you're wanting to talk to Doug Jr.'"

Rembrandt's eyes widened. "You asked his *father* to the dance?"

"I wanted to die, right then. I never talked to him again."

His laughter was deep and rich. It washed through her like summer rain.

"That is fantastic, Eve."

"Okay, what about you? What would you do over? Your regrets?"

His face turned solemn. He considered her for so long, she wanted to look away. His voice softened. "I think I would start all the good things sooner."

She frowned, "You're twenty-eight. What on earth could you start sooner?"

He didn't answer, just looked at her.

Her heartbeat pounded in her throat. *No.* She barely knew this man.

But she couldn't escape the sense that somehow she was part of his answer.

He got up, and took a step toward her, so much in his gaze it seemed to pin her to her chair, shuck away her breath. "Eve, I—"

The door slammed and steps sounded on the cement. She landed on her feet as if she might have been caught making out in the car, her heart thundering, her palms sweaty.

What now?

Silas slid into view. "I got the test results of that cup back." He wore his backpack over his shoulder, and frowned only for a moment after his gaze landed on Rembrandt.

He'd edged over to the table and was looking at the bomb fragments.

"And?"

"They belong to Ramses Vega, that guy who—"

"—I ran down today," Rembrandt finished, jerking his head up. He snapped to look at her. "What cup?"

"We found it on a side street near yesterday's bombing."

"What side street?"

She walked over to the table with yesterday's sketch of the crime scene. "Here. Across the street to the northeast, in front of the grocery store."

He stared at the map, then, "Do we have a map of the area?"

"I think so." She had used a city map to construct the former location and grid of the Daily Grind. Now, she pulled it out and unrolled it onto the table. Rembrandt leaned over it, searching for—

"Here. It's the Immigrant Learning Center." He trailed his finger south, along Nicollet Avenue. Tapped it. "If Ramses was on his way to school, he would have been heading the opposite direction. Instead, you found the cup here, across the street from a bus stop. Even if he was waiting for the bus, the next stop lets off another block further from the ILC. It's closer to walk."

Rembrandt grabbed his jacket. "I think we need to take another look at Ramses."

Litter fell out of his pocket and he reached down to pick it up.

Eve caught his arm. "What is that?" It looked like burlap. She eased it from his hand, "What are you doing with this? This is evidence. From yesterday's bombing." She set it on the table, and tried to keep accusation from her voice. "Where did you get this?"

"I picked it up on the street. *Today.*"

Oh. She really couldn't have missed this, could she? Eve pulled on her gloves and flicked on a light, reached for her magnifying glass and held the scrap under it for inspection. "See these three green leaves, these two brown dots? This is the logo for Green Earth coffee. The same coffee that Daily Grind uses."

She motioned with her head and Rembrandt followed her over to the body of evidence, cataloged and labeled from the Daily Grind fire. She found the appropriate bag and handed it to him. "See the logo?"

He stared at it, then looked up at her and a slow, almost languid smile slid across his face. "I could kiss you," he said softly.

Oh. *Oh.*

He put the baggie down, set his jacket back on the chair and said, "We're going on a bean hunt."

CHAPTER 15

I'm rewriting history.

That's my only explanation for the fact we've found a twenty-year-old lead to a case I'd poured over a hundred times.

The thought has me buzzing, as if I've downed too much coffee, jittery and on fire. I'm not sure why we never saw the connection before, but I can't ignore the old rush of a hot theory filling my veins.

"Let's Google it," I say, holding up the baggie with the burlap label, and when Eve just looks at me, I realize I've made yet another time-warp blunder.

Not unlike my suggestion for a digital facial recognition search. Good job, Slick. I'm not sure how much of my inadvertent future knowledge will affect the past, or, *uh*, the future. Except, now might be the time to invest in Google stock, right? Too bad they don't exist yet.

Eve shoots me an appropriately odd look. "Do what?"

I rack my brain for a few seconds. "I mean Yahoo."

She frowns but nods. "Sure. Yahoo."

She pulls up a chair to a desktop computer stationed in a nearby cubicle and I flip around a folding chair and straddle it, leaning on the back.

I can feel the heat of the spark still lingering between us, the one I lit with my words, *"I think I would start all the good things sooner."*

For a crazy second, the smell of her, the look in her eyes, something of surprise, even hope, ignites a different sort of buzz under my skin. Because I *know* that look. It's the same expression I get when she puts down her book, late at night, when she just wants me to ease away the ache of the day.

It's the hint of vulnerability Eve so rarely shows. The hard-wrought intimacy we fought to find after our many dating starts-and-stops.

However, while my twenty-eight year old body stirs with the memories in my head, in that moment it's the fifty-two year old, well-married man inside me that longs to wrap my fingers through her hair, pull her close, anchor myself to something familiar.

Something known. Something mine. No. Ours.

Except for Silas. His timely appearance brought me up short, reminded me that Eve is not mine. Yet.

She's young and eager, still relatively innocent and I am, in experience, if not in body, a much older man.

Which makes my impulses suddenly awkward and not a little creepy, and I'm possessed with the strangest urge to protect her.

From myself.

This is really getting weird.

She searches for Good Earth coffee and finds a listing. Not a website, apparently the world isn't quite that sophisticated yet, but a piece of data with relevant info.

"The company is located in Brazil, with distribution world-wide," Eve says, reading from the site.

"There has to be a connection," I say, not because it's such a rare and unique deduction, but I'm reaching a point of desperation. "It's our only known link between the two bombings."

I don't continue my thought that it's also the only link to tomorrow's horror. Unfortunately, yesterday's search didn't raise even a sliver of memory.

At this rate, I'll need some kind of miracle to stop tomorrow's bombing.

If I even can. Because suddenly every time paradox I've ever read whirls through my brain.

Is my failure already written into the timeline, no more than fated scenes about to play out and etched in stone? Or, can I stop it, and if so, does all of history change? Will I wake up to a new life tomorrow?

That brings me to the conundrum that I might actually be stuck here, right? How does one return to their time when they don't know how they got here in the first place? Art said only, *I think so,* to my question. I don't know about you, but in my book that isn't the reassurance I was hoping for. My watch is still ticking, so, that has to mean something, but what if I'm stuck here forever?

I'll be smarter. And richer. And maybe I'll enjoy it better this time around, so I guess I'm not horrified by this idea.

Except … what happens to Eve, in the future? *That* future. The one I vanished from without a trace. If I never get back, she'll never know what happened to me. Just like we never knew what happened to Mickey for so many years.

My hands grow clammy.

Then one more thought strikes me like a bolt of cold lightning.

Ashley.

I want them both back now, and that thought puts a fist right through my sternum so hard I nearly gasp.

I have to get back. I *will* get back.

But while I'm here, I'll save a few lives. In fact, the first thing I'll do after stopping this bombing is figure out how to get Danny Mulligan to stop hating me.

For no reason, I might add. His words to me, out of Eve's earshot, have left a bruise. *"I don't trust you, Stone, and I'm warning you—stay away from my daughter, unless it's work related. I don't want you to get her into trouble."*

Everything for the rest of my life will be classified as work related, you can bet on it. But I would really prefer Mulligan to like me, especially since he's going to be sticking around.

How? I'll figure that part out later.

I reach over Eve's shoulder and point to a listing down the page. "What is that article about a protest?"

It's something from a Canadian news site about an organized protest. Eve reads it as fast as I do.

"It looks like Good Earth coffee was named by the protesters as one of the perpetrators of child labor," she says, summing up what I've just read. "There's a long list."

"Who are the protesters?"

"A conglomerate group. The article mentions Free the Children, a couple church groups, and the International Child Labor Defense League."

"Yahoo that." That sounds weird. Apparently "Google it" doesn't translate. "Search for the Child Labor Defense League," I say, simplifying.

She's already typing it in and a few hits come up. "It's a group out of DC. They've been involved in a number of protests around the country. Here's one in Oregon, and another in New York City."

She pulls up the article. "Oh, wow, they're not exactly peaceful. Seattle. The burning of…a *coffee* shop."

"Was anyone arrested?" I'm reading it too, but Eve's always been a faster reader than me.

"A couple people. Gus Silva and…Jo De Paulo."

"Do a search—"

But she's already typing, and there is a hit for a Gustavo Silva, Brazilian footballer.

Brazilian.

"He immigrated to the US a year ago with D.C. United," Eve says. "And was arrested about three months later."

I sit back and shake my head. "What is a Brazilian footballer doing hooked up with a child labor protest group in Seattle?"

"According to the Child Labor Defense League, Brazil is one of the leading countries that uses child slave labor to pick their beans."

"Interesting. Where is Gustavo from in Brazil?"

"There's a picture of his team." She's pulled up the team roster. "Wow, about half these guys are international." She is scrolling down and right about the middle of the page, my gut clenches.

"Stop." I point to the screen. "That's Ramses."

"The guy you chased today?"

I nod and it's all I can do to sit here, every corpuscle in my body on fire. "I knew it."

"You think he's involved with the Child Labor Defense League?"

"He and Gustavo."

She has clicked on Gustavo's picture, and is reading his stats. "He's from a village in the State of Espirito Santo…" She clicks on Ramses pictures. "Bingo. Same as Ramses."

"They knew each other in Brazil."

She's typing again, and the awkwardness of feeling older, even more experienced is starting to dim, flushed away by that familiar, sweet jazz we get when we're onto something.

"The State of Espirito Santo is the biggest producer of Robusta coffee beans in the world."

"So these two boys escaped, through soccer. Except, why would Mariana not bring her son with her when she left Brazil?"

Eve looks at me. "Who?"

"Ramses's mother. Mariana Vega. I know she is divorced, but—"

"Mariana Vega. Of the Vega Family coffee growers?" She is pointing to a listing on the original protest site. "What if she couldn't bring him?" Eve turns, her hazel-green eyes alight. "I've heard stories of drug lords keeping mothers from seeing their children, from immigrating."

"Eve, you're brilliant," I say, and it's a such an easy, common word between us that it takes me by surprise when her eyes widen, a smile tipping her lips.

It hits me that this is the first time she's heard that from me and my throat thickens because I'm realizing that I'm not only rewriting the bombings.

Eve really likes me. The spark in her eye is easy, the smile lit with something inviting and if I'm reading her right—and let's not jump to any conclusions because I don't have the most attuned emotional barometer—I've somehow accelerated our romance by about a year.

Hooyah.

I'm trying not to act on the pulse between us. "It's not a difficult leap to suggest that Gustavo had friends—or even family—pressed into the coffee bean labor pool. And maybe Ramses saw it. Maybe he even became sympathetic to Gustavo's point of view."

"Maybe Gustavo recruited him for the Child Labor Defense League."

"But why is Ramses *here,* in Minneapolis, and not playing on the team?"

She clicked on his photo. "He's on the injured list."

"He didn't look injured when he was doing his 100 meter sprint today. See if you can find out anything else. I think it's time I have another chat with Mariana and her son."

Just like that, as if I can hear it, something clicks inside my brain.

Maybe I never heard of Ramses because he was killed in the third bombing. A voyeur to his own crime, drawn in too close to the flames.

"I heard Booker tell you to stay away from her." Eve looks at me, but as soon as the words are out of her mouth, she bites her lip. "I mean—sorry."

She has a point. More, probably Ramses isn't going to give up anything—not unless I haul him down to the precinct for a face to face. It's a good bet Mariana won't open her door to me. And, I'm not getting a warrant after today's tackle.

"He didn't tell Burke to stay away, though." I pull out my cell phone and Burke is on speed dial. He's grouchy and not a little irked that I abandoned him this afternoon—an opinion he didn't spare when I returned, two hours later, the meeting in Stillwater spinning in my head.

The watch is working.

155

Whatever. Right now, all I know is that my instincts are also working, and I ignore Burke's late night ire and update him on what Eve and I have found.

"It can't wait until morning?" he asks, and for a moment, I'm stymied.

He's already suspicious of me. *How did you know?* The memory of his disbelief, his fury this morning punches through my thoughts.

I don't know how long I'm going to be trapped here, and frankly the last thing I need in my suddenly off-kilter world is to lose Burke's trust. Still, we're running out of time. "What if Ramses is on the run? Or worse, planning to hit another coffee shop. Maybe even tomorrow morning?"

I don't *sound* desperate, so that's good, but I let the question linger in the quiet.

It also occurs to me that if we have Ramses, and he's our bomber, then the nightmare is over.

"I just got home from a gig."

Right. Burke is still a jazz drummer, even in my time, but now he's playing for a band that is making a name in Minneapolis. Someday, Sticks, as he's called, will have to make a choice between his police work and his music.

You know what he chose. So maybe that's why he's not a fan of *my* creative choice. I hadn't really considered that before.

Still, "Then I'm not interrupting anything. Get up and do me a solid, bro. Just go pick him up. I'll meet you at the station."

I am not sure if that is a curse I hear, but he mumbles something and hangs up.

"I did a check on the US distributor of Good Earth coffee. It's out of Chicago, but their offices are closed."

"I need a list of coffee shops that use this brand." I shake my head. "We could use a hacker."

She laughs. "Right. You and my brother—he's always trying to 'hack' into things. This isn't the movies, Rem."

I didn't know that about Asher. But then again, he died before he could show the world who he was.

Not this time.

My phone buzzes. It's Burke, texting to tell me that he's on his way to Ramses' house.

I glance at the clock. After eleven. We have eight hours, if my sketchy memory is even remotely correct.

Eve stands up. "I'm heading home, but let me know how it goes with Ramses."

I stop myself from reaching out and tugging on a strand of that twisty red hair, and instead nod. I grab my jacket and am about to start searching the city's coffee shops when Burke texts me again to meet him at the precinct office.

The parking lot is dark save for the puddle of light from the overhead streetlight. Moths dart through the glow, shadows against the pavement. The air is balmy, seasoned with a hint of freshly mowed grass and the slightest tinge of late night moisture. A breeze lifts my shirt.

I'm leaning against my car when lights stripe the lot and I make out Burke's Integra. He pulls up behind me, not in a space, and leaves the car running.

His expression is gnarled and edgy when he gets out, and it occurs to me that maybe I did interrupt something.

Naw. Burke is even more of a loner than I am. He works out, reads, and come to think of it, loves time travel books.

Ironic.

"What?" I ask, before he can attack.

"He's not there." He shuts the door to his still running car.

"What—?"

"The house was lit up, so I knocked, and Mariana Vega answered the door. Said Ramses had gone out—she didn't know where."

I stifle a curse but Burke frowns at me. "So we get him tomorrow—"

"No, we gotta stake out his house, grab him the second he gets back."

Burke is giving me a look like he did this morning, or even last night. "What's going on, Rem?"

Doggone it. "I just think…it's a—"

"I swear to you if you say this is a hunch, you'll lose teeth."

I close my mouth. Finally, "I was right last night. Why won't you just trust me?"

I've done it now, because I just might be the *only* person Burke trusts. And he has his reasons, but I know I've delivered a jab.

"Fine." His mouth tightens "Let's go."

"No. I have to…well, I have to figure out how to hack into a database in Chicago."

Burke just stares at me. Shakes his head.

Gets in his car without a word.

And I point my Camaro toward a little bungalow on Webster Ave South.

CHAPTER 16

You're brilliant.

Eve didn't know why those words lit up her entire body—Rembrandt probably meant it as a throw away comment, something he might say to Burke, or even Silas if he helped him track down a lead.

So she should simply calm down. Stop thinking about the way he straddled that chair, his forearms ropy and strong, resting on the back. The way he leaned past her, pointing at the screen, surrounding her with his scent—a mix of the sultry summer air and a thoroughly masculine residue of his morning exertions. Stop thinking about the softening timbre of his voice when he looked at her as if seeing her for the first time and said, *I think I would start all the good things sooner.*

All the good things.

As if they included her.

I could kiss you.

He hadn't meant that, either, but the shock of those words still sluiced through her.

She turned off the shower and let her body shiver for a moment before she stepped out and grabbed a towel. The weariness of the day had sloughed off her, but she still longed for her warm bed, if she could get her brain to shut off.

Tracking down the leads with Rembrandt only stirred up more questions. Like, where in Ramses' or even Gustavo's resume did it mention familiarity with bomb making procedures? More likely, they'd befriended someone inside the ICDL who could handle explosives.

Maybe they needed to take another look at the ICDL, something she'd mention to Rem—Inspector Stone—in the morning.

Despite what he said, she needed to stop thinking of him as Rem. As if they were more than work acquaintances. She couldn't deny that something about him, however—an aura of confidence, even the brazen courage to run after his hunches—nudged at a place inside her that longed to step outside her methodology and lists to follow her instincts.

What would you regret?

His question rattled inside her as she pulled on a pair of sweatpants, a T-shirt, and fuzzy socks for her perpetually frozen toes and headed downstairs to her freshly tiled kitchen. A light glowed over the stove and she opened the refrigerator. One of her brother's beers remained, but she grabbed a yogurt and headed over to the counter to fetch a spoon.

The knock at the door made her jerk. She turned. Glanced at the clock. After midnight.

She slowly slid out the drawer at the end of the counter and eased out her police-issue Glock.

Not that a criminal would knock, but...

Holding it at her side, she flicked on the porch light. Her brother had suggested a stained glass door, so she couldn't make out the figure standing there.

She glanced through the sidelight window.

A man. He had his back to the door, but wore a pair of dress pants, no jacket, his shirt sleeves rolled up, wide shoulders, lean waist—

"Inspector Stone?" She opened the door and he turned.

The shadows of the overhead light against the two-day growth of his whiskers turned his face gritty, and the look in his blue eyes suggested all business. He glanced at the Glock in her hand and raised an eyebrow.

"Okay, good idea. For the record, I like the preparedness, but I promise I'm not here to attack you, rob you, or in any way cause trouble." His mouth cranked up one side.

She glanced at the gun, then set the weapon on a table by the door. "It's late. So—"

"Like I said, good choice. Keep that instinct. But...I need your help, Eve." He stuck his hands into his pockets and then gave her such a sheepish, almost boyish look she didn't know what else to do.

"Come in."

He stepped over the threshold. "Nice place. Smells like you've been working on it."

"Yeah. My brother just finished the kitchen, but I'm about done with remodeling. I just need to paint the dining room and add a deck." She walked past him and turned on a family room lamp. Light washed over her leather sofa, across to her fireplace. "I'll be happy if I never remodel again."

A low chuckle rumbled through him. "I'll remember that."

The way he said it made it sound like they were already friends, and would be for a long time. She turned, her gaze quick over him. He stood in her entry way, watching her, and his shoulders lifted and fell, his expression suddenly awkward, as if realizing he had bridged the line between work and her personal life.

In fact, wait— "How did you know where I live?"

He lifted one side of his mouth. "Eve. I'm a detective."

Oh. Right.

Something she couldn't identify slipped into his gaze and she was suddenly, keenly aware of the fact that indeed, he'd stepped over that line, *right into her living room.*

Oh boy. "How did it go with Ramses?"

"He's out of pocket. Burke is staked out at his house, but…I gotta get into that data base of distributors of Good Earth coffee in our area."

"Tonight?" She didn't mean it quite how it sounded, but—

"I know it sounds crazy, Eve, but I just…" The look in his eyes turned solemn, even a little fierce. "I just know that there will be another bombing in the morning, and we have to figure out *where.*"

It was how he said it, so much conviction, so much *oomph* in his voice, she felt it to her bones, adopted it and made it her own. "Okay."

"Okay?" He blinked at her.

"How can I help?"

He drew in a breath, as if surprised, but he had called her *brilliant.*

And sure, Rembrandt might be a little impulsive, maybe even had a dark side, but no one could accuse him of giving up. Or not caring about the people who had lost their lives—who *could* lose their lives—if the bomber wasn't found.

No wonder he never had any cold cases.

"I was thinking your brother—"

"Asher?"

"Can he really hack into websites?"

"I think so. But—"

"Is he still living with your parents?"

Now this was weird, because—

"You mentioned that he was younger than you, so I just assumed."

Oh. But he swallowed, rather oddly.

"Yeah, he's at home. I think. Probably."

"Let's go." He started toward the door.

"I'm in my pajamas."

He glanced at her. "Those are your pajamas? Trust me, you're fine."

Hmmm.

He opened the door. She took off her socks, slipped on flip flops and headed outside.

A black Camaro sat under the lights. The sight of it stirred a dangerous flame inside her. Like she might be in high school, sneaking out of—or in this case, into—her house.

She settled in beside him and as he turned the car over, a classic rock tune queued up. "Lonely People," by America.

He was drumming his fingers on the steering wheel as he headed towards Minnetonka.

"You know where my parents live, too?"

He glanced at her, then, a deer in the headlights expression. "Uh, no, I was guessing—"

"Don't give me that. You're a detective."

"Sorry."

"You're as bad as my dad. This is why I had no dates in high school. Dad did a background check on everyone."

"Everyone?"

"Maybe just the troublemakers."

"You like the troublemakers, Eve?"

Her eyes widened. "What? No."

He was grinning, though. 38 Special's "I Want You Back" came on and he started to hum.

"I prefer to stay out of trouble, thanks."

"Which is why you're here, about to sneak into your old house—"

"You asked me for a favor."

"Yes." He glanced at her. "Yes I did."

"I *don't* get into trouble."

"I know that." Still singing, still grinning.

Fine. "I was thinking about the coffee shop bombing, and I was wondering how Ramses or Gustavo might know how to build a bomb. What if they had an accomplice? Someone they met along the way that could add terror to their protests."

His smile faded and he nodded. "Yeah. That's another angle we need to take a look at. Maybe your brother can hack into the ICDL site and get a list of their members." He turned off Hwy 7, onto Vine Hill, then west on Cottagewood. Arching cottonwoods and poplars dissected the night sky, clear and dotted with stars. A golden moon hung over the lake as they turned onto her road. He dimmed his lights and pulled to the side of the road, across the street.

"Now what?" Eve asked.

"Now, we go in there and get your brother." He turned off the car.

"How?"

"Through the garage? Is your dad home? And now I'm having this creepy déjà vu high school flashback."

"Of what, sneaking into your girlfriend's house?" She didn't know why she asked that.

"Nothing that crazy—I was never big on overactive dads with baseball bats—just sneaking out of the house with the boys. You know, to climb the water tower, shoot BBs at the local squirrels."

"What?"

"Calm down—we always missed." His eyes shone, the moonlight casting over his face, turning it mysterious, shadowed, tempting. "I didn't have a girlfriend in high school."

"Not one?"

"I played football and…aw, I didn't really know what to say…" His smile faded.

Behind his eyes, she saw it. The wounds of his loss still open, enough to keep people at arm's length.

All except her. That fact twined through her, turned the air between them thick and sweet, tugging her in.

She could too easily fall for a guy *exactly* like Rembrandt Stone.

"Well, I didn't sneak out—or have any boyfriends sneaking in—so it's highly likely we're about to get busted."

"I'll take my chances." He got out, closing the door quietly behind him.

She came around the car and when he took her hand, the warmth of his grip only ignited the surge of electricity buzzing under her skin.

"Stay along the edge of the driveway and the motion detection lights won't flicker on."

"See, you *have* done this before," he said as followed her. The lights stayed off and they reached the garage door.

"Maybe you should stay here," she suggested

"I'm not afraid of your dad, Eve."

The man could quite possibly read her mind.

"But I am," she whispered and patted him on the chest. Was his heart racing?

So, not as calm as his voice let on. Interesting.

"Fine. Hurry. And if you need me, do something, like make a noise, or scream, or call my name—"

She pressed her hand to his mouth. "Shh." Then she let herself into the garage.

Funny how in the thick of night, the familiar seemed foreign, riddled with danger. She nearly tripped over the lawn mower and right into a box of Christmas decorations. But she brailed her way to the back door, eased it open, and reminded herself to mention to her mother, sometime, casually, to lock the garage door at night.

The refrigerator hummed and she tiptoed through the kitchen, then up the stairs, avoiding the third step, right side, then into the hallway and right to her brother's bedroom.

His light was off, but when she opened the door, he looked up from where he sat at his desk, the glow of his computer screen lighting his face, bulky earphones cutting off any sound. She put a finger to her mouth and shut the door.

"What?" he whispered as he pulled off his earphones.

"I think I need your help." She eased over and glanced at some sort of computer game on the screen. "Can you really hack into things?"

He frowned. "Why?"

"I need help with a case. Hacking into a database in Chicago to get a list of addresses of local coffee shops that carry a particular coffee."

"Really?" His voice raised a little. "Does this have to do with the bombings?"

She again pressed her finger over her mouth. "Can you do it?"

"Sure," he turned to his computer.

"Can you do it from *my* computer?"

He considered her a moment, then scrubbed a hand over his face. "Yeah. I think so."

"Stay behind me, and don't make any noise," she said, but he stopped her with a hand to her arm.

"Sis. You're talking to the master. Watch and learn."

She might not know Asher as well as she thought. They were outside in moments, going out his upstairs window, onto the roof and climbing down a ladder conveniently—and possibly permanently—propped against the roof.

"Dad thinks I'm working on the gutters. Summer project." He winked as he followed her toward the garage.

Rembrandt emerged from the shadows. Held up a hand as Asher spotted him. "I'm with Eve."

She sort of liked how he said that.

"Nice wheels," Asher said as he climbed into the Camaro.

Rembrandt's voice filled the car, a delicious tenor as he sang along to a song from Steve Miller's "Fly Like an Eagle."

They pulled up to her dark house and she led Asher into her den, firing up her computer.

Rembrandt stood behind them, watching.

Eve gave Asher the rundown of the case, what they'd found, and when he pulled up the distributor's site, he shooed them out of the room. "I could use a pop, though."

She fetched it, then found herself sitting on the counter in the kitchen, watching Rembrandt drink the beer Samson had left in her fridge.

He leaned against the opposite counter. Glanced at the clock.

"You really think another bomb is going to go off?" she asked, studying the little pucker of worry between his eyes.

He nodded. "Bombings are designed to make the news, to scare people out of their normal routines and to make a point. I think we're onto something with this ICDL group. The first one got our attention. The second scared us into staying away from coffee shops. A third one alerts us to their mission and makes us sit up and listen. Their threat is not only credible but irrefutable. They want to force people to pay attention. Yeah, there's another one coming. And I can't live with myself if we don't stop it." He stared at his beer. "I don't want it haunting me for the rest of my life."

The way he said it, goosebumps lifted on her skin.

"I was thinking about what you said at lunch about regretting things...yes, I'd want to save my friend, but maybe if I did, I would have never become a CSI. And then...well, I might end up being, I don't know, a doctor, or even, a *barista*. I could have been one of those victims at the coffee shops."

He looked up at her.

"I'm just saying that if we did everything differently, we'd still have to learn the same lessons, somehow, right? And if we didn't, maybe one small change would make everything different. Even, much, much worse."

She wasn't sure where that philosophy came from. "I guess I just think that everything happens for a reason. And going back to change it would mean we'd be a lesser person for the lack of the lesson."

He looked at her, nodding quietly, his blue eyes in hers, as if hanging onto her words.

The expression threaded through her, tugged, and maybe that's why she slid off the counter. Why she walked over to him.

He watched her the entire way, his gaze on her turning warm, hot. He swallowed, his breaths rising and falling.

She hesitated only a moment before she put her hands on his chest. Contoured, warm, his heartbeat pounded under her hand.

He set his beer on the counter beside him.

"Eve," he said quietly, his voice more of a whisper.

"Everything happens for a reason, Rembrandt. Like you appearing on my doorstep tonight." Her pulse thundered in her ears, her words crazy, daring. *You like the troublemakers, Eve?*

No. Just this one.

So, before her common sense could grab a hold, she rose up on her tiptoes, caught his eyes—

He took a breath in, and his hand tangled into her hair. "I like your hair down..."

Aw. She simply couldn't—or didn't want to—stop herself. Maybe driven by the impulse, the uncanny sense that she belonged, somehow, in Rembrandt's arms, and he, in hers...she kissed him.

For a moment, he didn't move, didn't even breathe. And for a split second, a fear sliced through her that—

Um no. Because just like that, he came alive. He pulled her into himself, kissing her like he'd been holding his breath, waiting. As if, like her, the urge had lingered in the back of his mind for two days.

He tasted of the beer he'd been drinking, and her body responded, leaning into his exploration.

She hadn't kissed many guys in her life—few, actually—but she knew the difference between a fumbling boy and a man who knew what he was doing.

It sent a dangerous, delicious spark through her. Troublemakers, indeed.

Rembrandt Stone. She wrapped her arms up, around his shoulders, closed her eyes, and a small, intimate humming sound emerged.

It only ignited a tiny growl from the back of his throat.

Apparently Inspector Rembrandt Stone was all business, whether he was solving crimes or making a move. Strangely, deliciously, he kissed her almost like he *knew* her, maybe better than she knew herself, his kiss soft, then deepening, then again lingering, making her ache for more.

This man. Her fingers played with the button of his dress shirt, then found his hot skin and the fine hairs of his chest. Yes, she heard the sirens, sensed the dangerous pull of him, but now ignited, she hadn't the power to stop.

Didn't want to. Because something about his intoxicating presence made her feel alive, brave and yes, even brilliant. Every part of the person she longed to be.

"Okay, I think I figured it out—Whoa!"

Her brother came skidding into the room and Rembrandt jerked away from her, his hands on her arms to steady her.

"Sorry!" Asher turned, about to exit—

"No, it's okay, Ash—" she started, but Asher had already fled. She laughed.

Not Rembrandt. His eyes widened and something that looked horribly like guilt flashed across his face. "Um...I..."

Oh, for Pete's sake, they weren't teenagers. "Take a breath, Rem." She patted his chest, then pushed him away, completely aware that her wet hair lay in tangles, her skin probably flushed red, and surely anyone could see her pounding heartbeat.

Still, no regrets here.

"What did you find, Ash?" She followed him into the den, keenly aware of Rembrandt behind her, and when Ash sat down at the computer, she noticed Rem run a hand behind his neck, glance over at her, then away.

Rembrandt Stone looked suspiciously like he might be freaking out.

Huh.

So maybe the guy didn't break the rules often either. So much to learn about him.

Rem crossed his arms over his chest, planted his feet and stared at the screen, at the listing of stores, with addresses.

"There are five stores that carry this coffee in the Metro area," Asher was saying. "Two, of course, are the locations of the previous bombs, but there are three more, two in Minneapolis, one in St. Paul."

"Can you print out the addresses?" Rembrandt said, his tone now all business.

"Sure." Asher hit the print button and Rembrandt walked over and stood over the printer, as if he could magically make it print by glaring at it.

Asher glanced at her, grinned. Eve hit him on the back of the head.

The printer spit out the list and Rembrandt took it. Returned to Asher.

"Okay, now I need you to hack into the International Children's Defense League and see if you can get me a list of names."

Asher lifted an eyebrow. "Um, if it has private donors, it'll be an encrypted site. It'll take time."

"How much time?"

"Hours. Days, even."

By the look on Asher's face—

"You don't know if you can do it," Eve said.

Asher shrugged. "I'll try."

Rembrandt checked his watch, something that looked like an antique. She'd noticed it the first day—and the fact that John Booker had one that looked just like it. Must be a department thing.

"It's after 3 am. I'd better get you home, kid."

That was probably the right decision. But she glanced at Rembrandt, searching for something that might indicate he was coming back...

He didn't look at her, staring at the printout.

Okay, and now they were back in middle school.

Asher got up and headed to the door.

She caught Rembrandt's arm, and he turned. Barely met her eyes.

"What's going on?"

He drew in a breath. Then, oddly, lifted his gaze to hers, reached out and touched her cheek. He drew his thumb down it in a caress, a gesture so sweet it left her wordless.

"I don't want any more regrets," he said quietly.

Then he walked out the door behind Asher, and closed it.

CHAPTER 17

Maybe I haven't been completely clear about the way things were between Eve and I, the first time through. The fact is that we didn't exactly hit it off right away. Sure, I brought her coffee, offered to pay for her busted camera, but like I said, I wasn't all that bright back then and it didn't occur to me to ask her out for at least two months. And even when that did finally happen, it was just the first step on a long road.

I liked her, sure, but during that season she was trying to track down her father and brother's murderer, and although we worked together, flirted, downed a few after work beers and occasionally found ourselves folded together on her sofa, we dodged any commitment for a couple of years.

Then came my undercover years, and that's another story, but it's hard to love a man you hardly see, and when he does finally turn up, he looks like he's just escaped from a maximum security prison, and tells tales that are straight out of an FX television series.

Let's just say that Eve had her reasons for not wanting to tie herself to a guy like me.

And then there was Silas. Always in her ear, whispering that I was trouble. He was probably right, but it didn't help our relationship.

Eve would argue with me, but I always suspected he was holding a torch for her.

Yet, despite Silas, despite the demons that kept me on the run, Eve and I kept finding each other, drawn by something bigger than ourselves, our fears, insecurities and even vices. We understood each other, more than anyone else in our lives could, and at the end of the day, respected each other.

Eve was my compass, my anchor to a life I desperately longed for, even if I didn't know it.

I was the gasoline to the fire simmering inside her.

I'd forgotten how dangerous that combination could be until tonight when she stepped up to me, studied me with those luminous hazel-green eyes, holding more promise than she could even imagine, and kissed me.

I tried—really, with everything inside me, you have to know I tried not to kiss her. Because, awkwardly, *my* Eve, the one I was desperate to get back to, was in my head calling me a cheater. Yeah, I know. Weird. But the truth is, this Eve is not my Eve. Not yet. So maybe I am cheating.

But as her soft lips found mine, her aroma rising around me, everything merged into one succinct emotion. My Eve became *now* Eve, the gentle curl of her hair falling over my fingers, the taste of her filling every barren crevasse as she kissed me.

How could I not kiss her back? Yeah, I agree, I lost myself there, every thing about her so familiar. It took over and pushed me somewhere I know she wasn't ready for. God help me, but in that moment, every crazy nuance, every unbelievable event of the past thirty-six hours broke open and for a few sweet moments that ached soul deep, I was home.

I'm still shaking a little, my hands tight on the wheel, the fragrance of Eve still haunting, distracting me as I drive Asher home. The night is thick, my lights peeling back the darkness as we ride down the highway.

Asher says nothing as he sits beside me, tapping his hands on his jeans. I should turn on the radio, something to fill the prickle of silence between us.

I don't remember Asher at all. From Eve's stories, he was smart, a little bit of a renegade and her favorite. Wiry, this Asher has Eve's dark auburn curls, his hair surfer long. Our daughter, Ashley, despite her wispy blonde hair, is his ironic spitting image. Tonight he's wearing a black Guns N' Roses T-shirt, a pair of cargo shorts, and high top Cons.

"So, you're into my sister, huh?" he says into the darkness, apparently not able to stand the void.

Your sister is my entire life. I don't say that, though. Instead, "I'd appreciate it if you just forgot what you saw tonight. At least for now." I look at him. "We need to figure things out."

My own words make me want to wince, the line feeling fresh off the set of *Friends*. But he lifts a shoulder. "I don't care. It's your funeral."

I frown, but I don't exactly want to know what he means, so I flip on the radio.

Oh great, a little Bad Company rolls on with *Feel Like Makin' Love.*

Great.

He's looked out the window and I think I see a grin.

I flick off the radio and pull onto his street. Stop a few doors down. "Thanks."

"No problem, dude." He gets out, slams the door and disappears into the night.

I wait a few minutes, just in case there's shouting, then head back to Uptown.

I don't want any more regrets.

My own words are in my head, and I roll down the window, letting the night wind sweep over me, dislodge the carnal desires still stirring inside. I meant it when I said I wish I could do things differently with Eve, get rid of the myriad stops and false starts, but this isn't quite what I was thinking.

Okay, fine. I admit that's exactly what I thought for a few minutes there, but now that I'm *here*, I'm afraid of screwing things up. Again.

And, what I neglected to mention is that time seemed to be looping back around to a familiar song between Eve and me. Late night case, a beer in the kitchen, the sultry summer night wind teasing the curtains at the windows. More than once we let things spill over from the kitchen to her living room, then upstairs to her bedroom.

That's a couple years away, really, but it started a cycle that we couldn't break, the hot-cold, on again, off again torrid romance that nearly did us both in. Eventually Ashley arrived. To my great regret, I still had to think about what to do as Eve handed me the little white stick with the plus sign, as if marriage might be a noose that would cut off air to the rest of my life. Practical Eve suggested we didn't have to be married to make good parents.

But, like I said, Eve is my compass, my anchor, and it took the thought of some other man—and Silas came to mind—raising my daughter, holding the woman I love late at night and the right answer took hold.

I'd like to not have broken Eve's heart a few go-rounds before Ashley came along.

And okay, I'm a different man now, but like Eve suggested tonight, what if one small change makes everything worse?

What if I screw everything up again…and this time I run out of second, third, even fourteen (I lost count how many times Eve took me back) chances?

My head is pounding, the lateness of the hour, the beer, and even the list tucked into my back pocket of the three coffee shops with the Good Earth brand are aligning to make me want to go to my apartment, pull the covers over my head and wish to wake up. *Really* wake up and let it all be over.

To be tucked up beside Eve in our fixer upper craftsman, my muse a cement block in my head, our towheaded daughter across the hall wishing for her Gomer.

I'll live with my nightmares if I can just be assured that I haven't somehow screwed up everything I already have.

But I have a terrible gut feeling that if I do that, tomorrow I'll wake up to yet another morning with Burke pounding at my door, eight more lives lost.

I tap my breaks at the light and while I wait, I pull out the list. Like Asher said, three stores, one of them in St. Paul. I know that one is out because I remember the bombing happening on this side of the river.

So, that leaves the other two locations. I glance at the clock—a little before four a.m.

Time enough to do a drive by, see if anything jogs a memory.

I pass Webster with only a glance toward Eve's house. I can't see it from here, though, so I don't know if she's left a light on.

The thought makes my entire body ache as I turn off highway 7 onto 100 and head south to Bloomington.

177

The radio is no help to my decision. Aerosmith is singing *I Don't Want to Miss a Thing*.

It's a quick drive on the deserted highway, just a few cars out. I pass a couple of Minneapolis' finest idling under overpasses, remembering the speed limit these days is 55.

Highway 100 turns into Normandale, which turns into Old Shakopee Road and I head west, the area hazy in my memory. I'm not holding out hope for recognition.

CityPerk is located in a strip mall sandwiched between a Chinese takeout joint and an insurance company. I pull into the parking lot, staring at the green awning, the brick exterior, the metal chairs outside, the folded umbrellas and especially the darkened windows.

Nothing. Not a nudge, not an itch, it's as if I've gone to Taiwan for all the familiarity of the place. (I've never been to Taiwan, for those wondering).

The hours say 6 a.m.- 9 p.m.

It occurs to me that maybe I should check in with Burke. So, while I sit there, I call him.

He answers on the first ring, which tells me he's on the job, and not happy about it. "What?"

"So, no go on Ramses?"

"He's not here, probably picked up a girl and is getting a good night's sleep. Which is what I should be doing. Where are you?"

I give him a short rundown of my activities. To his credit, he's all, 'uh huh,' and 'interesting,' but when I finish with the fact I'm staking out one of the two locations, he's silent.

I know there is a *why* forming in his brain, but he doesn't want to say it. So I fill in for him. "On the off chance there's going to be a third bombing, I want to be prepared."

"You can't stake out every coffee shop in the city."

"No," I say, and I hold in the rest—the fact that if I'm at the right place, at the right time, this all ends. But I do add, "If, by a crazy chance, Ramses isn't sleeping off a hangover, and is in fact, on his way to deliver bomb number three, I plan to stop him."

Silence. Then, "Sure."

I don't expect that, but maybe Burke is still rattled by the deaths, the terrible task of informing families of the tragedy. It had to bring up his own not-so-quiet demons.

"What's the other location?"

I turn on my dome light and read the address. "It's downtown. CityPerk, on 10th Ave. In the warehouse district, by the river."

"I'll meet you there if Ramses doesn't show up by 6 a.m."

I agree, hang up, and pull out of the lot, back onto Old Shakopee Road, winding my way back to the city. Minneapolis at this time of night has lost its allure. The bars are closed, the streets inhabited by the weary, the homeless and the soused. I take 35W into the city, veer onto 94 and get off on Washington Ave.

The Town Hall Brewery we ate at yesterday is only a couple blocks away, but it suddenly feels like years since I was there with Eve.

Driving southeast would bring me into the University of Minnesota campus and more memories, but I turn northwest, along the river, past the hotels, the warehouses that, over the next twenty years will turn into high-end flats, and finally all the way to 10th Avenue.

The shop is located on a soon-to-be revitalized vintage brick building, just down the road from the Minneapolis Public Works offices and across the street from a vacant warehouse.

I'm starting to get my bearings. Now, and I mean in *my* now, in the stead of the warehouse stands a five-story parking garage.

I have a feeling I know why.

Because more is coming back to me. The coffee shop is the last in a line of tiny local shops, a florist, a bicycle repair shop, a café, and just down the street, an eclectic gym. They're all located on the bottom level of a massive, empty warehouse. I'm standing in the middle of time here, that crest of hope that if you build it they will come. I have no doubt some contractor somewhere is drawing out plans for 900 square foot, open-beamed lofts.

I get out and stand under the streetlight, getting a feel for the place. Maybe it's the darkness, almost like the edge of a dream, but I can almost smell it, the singe of flame against wood, hear the shatter of glass.

I make out faded lettering on the brick above the shops. A store supply center. Store supply means displays, racks and…mannequins.

I see them in memory, just a flash through the back of my mind. Charred, their faces distorted, curled into themselves from the heat. Bodies that lay grotesquely on the pavement, jarring us into panic until we realize the truth.

Bingo.

I was here. I stood outside the rim of fire, watching the water arc, listening to the chaos.

Eight people died. But worse, this time the bomber hadn't spared the nearby buildings. Whether too enthusiastic, or simply unaware, he'd created a force that leveled almost half this city block.

The reminder turns me ill and I bend over, gripping my knees, my stomach roiling. But it's empty, save for the beer, so I gulp in breaths and clear my head before I make a fool of myself on the street.

I climb back into my car, sweaty, trembling.

This time, no one will die.

I back up, out of the light, swaddled in the darkness with a good view of the shop, lay my head back on the rest, pin my eyes on the store, and wait.

CHAPTER 18

It always starts the same way. I'm standing in the middle of a lake—not a big lake, more of a bay, with a wooden bridge arching over a waterway into the larger expanse.

This lake is surrounded by cattails and rushes frozen in January's grip, some broken, turned mustard and brown in the crisp air. A thin layer of snow casts over the ice, thick and blue and rippled by the wind. People often believe ice freezes in pristine, skate-able smooth sheets when in fact it is scarred with thick runnels and often littered with the carcasses of unfortunate ducks and geese, trapped in its frozen grasp.

My breath puffs out smoky, then clears in the frigid air. I can almost feel it—the numbing grip of the below-zero temperature stinging my nose, but as dreams go, I can't really feel anything. I can only hear. The wind, moaning through the willows and behind it a voice.

Always the voice, haunting, calling.

I turn, searching the shore. Empty. Just the skeletal arms of birch and poplar reaching to the gunmetal gray sky.

Then I hear the crack. It's sharp, like a shotgun, fracturing the air, and although it's expected, I flinch. Ravens startle and lift from the rushes. The wind whips the snow into a dervish at my feet and only then do I think to look down.

A vein has fissured open below my feet.

I start to run.

I'm fast. I can feel it, running with my mouth open, breathing hard. I pump my arms, careening across the ice, but my feet betray me and I slip. I fall, slam hard. My wind explodes out of me.

Another crack, and this time the report shatters my bones. Shaking, I lift myself off the glass. The ice webs under my mittened hands.

As I scramble to my feet, I'm no nearer the shore.

Now, a voice is calling.

I'm gasping, my breath labored, fatigue weighting each step.

The cycle repeats. I run, I fall hard, and it knocks my world sideways. Then the crack, the voice and in my soul, I know I'll never reach shore.

The lake will open, and I'll slide into the dark, murky, frigid depths. Disappear.

They'll never find me.

Rembrandt!

I wake with a rush, as if the voice is right beside me and I'm trembling, my breathing rough. If I were at home, next to Eve, she would have her hand pressed to my chest, her voice in my ear. *It's just a dream.*

I lean my head back into my headrest. I might be able to travel through time, but clearly I've brought my demons with me.

Sweat slicks my body and I run my hand across my mouth, find it dry.

The dawn has peeled back the night, sun hovers just above the horizon, filtering light along the dusky streets. Gold dew speckles my windshield and a chill slinks through my car. June in Minnesota can still find the temperatures in the low sixties and I shiver, now free of the horror of the dream.

I need coffee. Ironic, I know, but I glance at the shop across the street, wondering if it's open.

The windows are dark. A car drives up and pulls into the alley, to what I assume is parking in the back.

I glance at the watch. A little after 5:30 a.m. It must be the owner, up at the crack of dawn to care for the early risers. The shop is still dark, the place locked up. I sit up, scrub a hand down my face, the other on the steering wheel. Burke hasn't called, and I pick up my phone just in case he texted.

Nothing.

Then it hits me.

5:30 a.m. *Up at the crack of dawn.*

Right now, my father is heading to the barn to feed and milk his small herd of dairy cows before he takes off for work.

Mom is in the kitchen, making his breakfast. By six a.m., Sheriff Rickland will have arrived, and with my father still in the barn, Rickland will accept the cup of coffee my mother offers.

But she's suspicious, and doesn't need to wait for my father to know the truth. She'll guess that Rickland is there with news of my brother's body recovery, and then time will repeat itself.

Her high blood pressure will burst a vessel in her brain, and she'll collapse with a hemorrhagic stroke.

Maybe it's just naive, but I've always believed that if my father—or I—had been with her, maybe the stress would have been easier to bear, and she wouldn't have collapsed.

Wouldn't today—or at least in *my* today—be walking with a cane, struggling to speak.

The light in the coffee shop flickers on.

The street is still empty. But I know, and it's not just my gut, but *history*, that tells me the bomber will be here. The bomb explodes shortly after 7 a.m. Before, I was in bed, sleeping.

Before, I was awakened by Burke.

Before, I didn't answer my father's frantic call as he rode in the ambulance with my mother because I was counting bodies outside 10th Avenue Brew.

I pick up the phone and dial, my gaze scanning the street. *Please.*

"Hello?" My mother's voice is cheery and for a few seconds, it jars me to hear it so pure, so unblemished.

I swallow, clear my throat. "Mom. It's me."

"Rembrandt. It's so early—are you okay?"

She doesn't mean to, but she wears in her voice the terrible fear that something might happen to her only remaining son. "I'm fine. Actually, I'm sitting outside a coffee shop, about to go to work, but…" And my brain is groping for something, *anything*— "Is Dad around?"

"He's on his way to the barn—"

"I need to talk to him."

"I'll tell him to call you back—"

"Mom?" My voice shakes a fraction. No one else would have noticed, but I know Mom does. I swallow again. "I need to talk to him *right now*."

She's quiet because we don't do big emotion in our family, but after a second, "All right. Hang on."

A car pulls up outside the shop and parks in front. A man gets out, in a pair of track pants, a T-shirt, running shoes, and I agree with him. Coffee before exercise, right? He carries nothing, so I let him go.

One minute, two, then, "Hello?"

My father is out of breath, and a streak of guilt goes through me. I don't want to lie, but I'm not sure what to say. *Stay with Mom.*

"Rem?"

"Hey, Dad."

"You okay?"

They were good parents to me, despite the grief, the complete shutdown of our family after Mickey went missing. And they never said it out loud—*you should have stayed with him. This is your fault.*

They didn't have to. It was carved into my DNA.

"I'm okay. But Dad—" I draw in a breath and say the only thing that makes sense. "Happy Birthday."

Silence.

"What?"

"It's your birthday today, right?" I'm grimacing.

"I guess so."

"Well, then, Happy Birthday."

And then, thank God, I hear my mother's voice in the background. "Vin, there's a police car pulling into the drive."

I lean my head back, my heart punching my sternum. "A police car?" I ask in my very best impression of light concern. "What's that about?"

"I'm not sure. Um. Thanks for calling, son."

"I'll be over as soon as I can," I say, but he hangs up.

I fight this crazy urge to weep for the pain they're about to experience. But I'm holding onto a feeble, impossible hope that this time, things won't end quite so badly.

Across the street, a bicyclist has pulled up, parked and has gone into the shop. It's still early, a little past 6 a.m.

Over an hour before the blast.

I want coffee. And I want to get eyes on the shop.

I get out and cross the street. Glass windows, a planter out front that overflows with geraniums. A sandwich board with specials sits just outside the door, calling people inside with freshly made butterscotch scones. My stomach is a monster.

The place is small, homey. Groupings of wicker chairs circle low round coffee tables, two slipcovered sofas facing each other, a blackboard with the menu chalked on it, the ceiling high and open to the pipes. Freshly roasted java seasons the air. I would have liked this place.

It's possible Ramses left a package here last night, so I look around. Three thermoses of coffee, their names hanging in tags are lined up along the bar, but I see nothing out of place. A middle-aged blonde, her hair tied back with a handkerchief and wearing a tie-dyed apron fills a glass case. Her name tag reads Katia.

I spot the scones. And a couple of old-fashioned donuts. And fresh pumpkin bread.

Yeah, I would have found a writing niche here. Maybe I will, someday.

"Can I help you?"

I study the board and decide on today's special, a macchiato. I order it with extra espresso.

The runner sits in the corner, reading a newspaper. He glances at me, and I notice he has blonde hair cut short, military style, and a tattoo peeks out of his shirt, on his upper arm. He looks away from me and stares into the paper.

The bicyclist is seated at the counter on a high top, talking to the barista. He has his dreadlocks pulled back into thick blonde chunks and is trying to bargain for a free donut.

Katia makes my coffee and I debate sitting inside or out, then decide to head back to the Camaro. If Ramses sees me it's possible he won't drop his bomb. Which, of course, saves lives, but also means that I'll be fresh out of historical leads. I realize I'm cheating, but like I said, I don't care.

I slide back into the Camaro, take a sip and nearly spill my macchiato down my shirt when knuckles rap on my passenger side window.

Burke.

I reach over and unlock the door and he folds himself inside.

"No luck with Ramses?"

He shakes his head, eying my coffee. "What are we doing here?"

"I have a hunch."

"Perfect." He closes his eyes, as if in pain.

I take another sip.

The street is coming alive. Another bicycler, and a car parks in front of the florist. A bus pulls up, coughs and eases to the curb at the end of the street. The neon light in the cafe flickers on and the sign is turned over.

Burke sighs, rubbing his finger and thumb into his eyes. "I need some coffee—Rem... *There he is.*"

I would have spotted him, given another second. He's gotten off the bus and stands at the stop, waiting to cross the road. Ramses is a handsome, unassuming bomber, wearing a gray T-shirt, a pair of jeans, tennis shoes. Brown hair, a hint of a beard, just a guy stopping in for coffee.

Burke reaches for the door handle.

"Wait. Let's see if he's carrying anything."

He is. A satchel over his shoulder. It bumps against his leg as he looks both ways, then treks across the street.

189

I set my coffee down. "Let's get him."

Burke is already out of the car, and I admit to a silent huzzah that he believes me. Because why else would Ramses be *here?*

I follow Burke out and we scuttle across the street, not wanting to alert Ramses before we can get close enough to grab him.

But also not wanting whatever is in that satchel to go boom.

Ramses is just about to reach the door when Burke calls his name.

There's a moment, a hiccup, when Ramses turns on instinct, when he sees Burke, then me, advancing on him.

He hesitates. I can almost read his mind.

It's over.

Or, he could die a martyr for his cause.

In a second he's swung the door open and disappears inside. I take off in a sprint, a plan forming. "Burke! Evacuate the coffee shop. I'm going around the back!"

I angle toward the alley, shooting past the door, but in a blinding second of terrible luck, it slams open.

I plow into the bicycler, and we sprawl together hard on the pavement.

"Hey!" he growls.

I glare at him and untangle myself, hoofing it around back.

I hear Burke, now inside the shop, yelling. Please, God, don't let Ramses pull a trigger.

I'll come in from behind and trap him.

I find the back door propped open. I sneak inside, picking my way past shelves of supplies—cups, napkins, sweeteners, bags of Good Earth coffee.

When I emerge, it's behind the counter and I spot Burke standing in front of Ramses, hands up, talking in low tones.

Ramses has—*you've got to be kidding me*—a gun. He's got Katia by the arm and holds his weapon against her head.

Burke is staying back, but I know he sees me.

And I smile.

Because I know exactly what to do, and I'm hoping, praying even, that Burke knows it too.

An imperceptible nod.

I move behind Ramses.

It happens in synchronicity, almost like a dance. But that's how we are, Burke and I. Partners. Brothers. We've always been able to read each other's minds.

He dives at Katia, tackling her away from the gun as I simultaneously grab Ramses and slam him onto the floor.

I haven't forgotten yesterday, the fact that he's big, wiry, and athletic. But don't forget I have that twenty-eight-year-old body.

I'm also big, wiry, and athletic.

We land together, and he elbows me, but I'm quicker. I dodge the attack, get a knee in his back and grab for his hand, hoping for a submission hold.

Not in time. He rolls, knees me and lands a blow in my gut. But I shake it off, and hit him with everything I have inside me. My fist meets his face and pain shudders through both of us.

He howls out a curse and grabs me around the neck, pulling me down.

But my fists are free and I land two solid shots in his ribs. He grunts.

I don't stop.

I know I should, but he's still holding me down, still writhing and I have twenty-four years of fury roiling through me. I reach for his free hand, but it's grappling for something between us.

"Rem!"

Burke's shout coincides with a blinding flash of pain in my side.

Ramses has gotten his hands on a knife and speared it into my side.

The pain takes me apart, blinds me, and I suck wind.

He pushes me off. But I still have hold of his satchel and heaven help me, I'm not letting go.

Then there's Burke. Where he's been all this time, I don't know, but as I grip the satchel with everything inside me, he trips Ramses, lands on his exposed back and gets him into that hold I longed for.

And I'm bleeding like a freakin' stuck pig.

I still have a hand on the satchel and I drag it off him, scoot back to the wall, forgetting for a second my wound as I scrabble for a look inside.

For once, I'm glad to be right. Inside is a metal cylinder, like a thermos, and my guess is it doesn't hold coffee.

My look of relief must transmit to Burke because he smiles as he begins to cuff Ramses.

"I told you to trust me," I mumble, but my voice is strained. I just need to lay down.

"Call 911!" he shouts to Katia and moves to catch me. "Rem, stay with me—"

The room spins and as I crumple to the floor, strange ringing sounds echo through the shop, almost like an alarm. Or, maybe sirens.

A loud wind bullies the room and finds my bones, thundering through me. Drowning me. Time, spinning up. I close my eyes, letting it take me.

Then everything around me shatters, and I'm falling.

Voices sound a short distance away, but muffled, and when I open my eyes, I half expect to see paramedics, or even the glare of an ER.

It takes me a long moment—blinking into the fading sunlight cascading across a desk, leather chair and credenza—to realize I'm back. In my office.

Back to the life I worried I might never return to.

I'm still clutching my side, and now sit up, expecting the pain to tentacle around me, cut off my breathing, blind me.

But it's vanished. I'm fine.

Not sitting in a pool of my own blood.

Not holding a satchel that contains a thermos filled with ammonium nitrate, fuel oil, and antimony sulfide.

Not watching Burke cuff Ramses Vega, the Coffee Shop Bomber.

My legs shake as I climb to my feet, my entire body trembling with the force of the dream. It *had* to be a dream, right? My empty whiskey glass sits beside my keyboard and I pick it up.

Smell it.

I don't feel drugged.

On the contrary, every nerve is lit, the layers of my subconscious alive and vivid in my mind.

I remember the smell of the night seeping into the Camaro, the salty taste of Eve's skin, the burn of Ramses's fist in my gut, the explosion of my knuckles against his face. I can describe in detail my old apartment, along with Eve's, and the expression on Booker's face as he watched the second bombing. I even remember Laurie Stoltenberg, the witness from the first bombing.

Rich, vivid details to an event that feels as if it happened yesterday.

The kind of details that belong in my book.

My muse is back with a fist pump, and it's lit my brain with what-ifs and twists.

An ending that just might work.

Voices draw me to the door, and I open it, listening.

The television. I picture Ashley, curled up on the sofa, where I left her, playing a video game, or maybe now she's watching one of her kids' shows. I debate going to her, pulling her into an embrace, but I know it'll lead to tickles and my hunkering down with her to watch something animated and I'll forget the muse for something richer.

I have a deadline, promises to keep.

I softly close my door.

I don't hear any of Eve's footsteps creaking across our bedroom above me which means she's probably out on her run. I check my watch.

Booker's watch. The hands are unmoving, stuck at three and seven, like before. I fiddle with the dial, but they remain lifeless.

Maybe it was all a dream.

My screen saver is spinning, so I return to my desk. I cap the whiskey bottle and shove it back into the drawer.

Powerful stuff, that Macallan.

Then, I pull up my manuscript.

The cursor is blinking, taunting.

But the muse is mine, and I'm right beside her as long as she wants to run.

***

Butcher found Gabby leaning over her microscope, her eye pressed to the lens, a dozen slides lined up beside her.

"Any luck?"

"You'd better have coffee when you slink in this late," she said, not looking up.

"Why aren't you at home?" He didn't mean his tone. It just wasn't always easy to keep his thoughts straight around Gabby. She wore her dark hair back in a ponytail, no makeup. Still captivating despite her shapeless medical garb.

"I found something." She got up and went over to a table of twisted black wiring, plastic and other bomb debris, all labeled.

"The bomb was on a timer. I found the remnants of an alarm clock. It's a simple design, but effective."

Butcher took it apart. "He planted it, then walked away to watch."

"Mmmhmm." She leaned a hip against the table. "So why do you think he watched?"

"A bombing is a particular kind of crime. It's not easy, building a bomb, and a bomber is a meticulous kind of person. He'd want to make sure it went off."

Butcher wished he'd brought her coffee now, because he liked the way her face lit up when he did. If he played his cards right, they could work all night.

"It gives them a sense of power," she said, riffing off his theory.

"Even vengeance. It satiates the frustration boiling up inside."

"What if it's all of the above?" Gabby said. "What if he's both meticulous *and* has an agenda? What if this is about changing the world, making it fit what he wants?"

"And he does this by destroying the thing he hates and starting over?"

"A clean slate," Gabby said. "He rebuilds the world as he sees it."

"Without the mistakes that were made the first time."

"Isn't that what 9/11 was about? Wanting to remake the world, starting with vengeance, then a takeover of the world with radical ideology?"

I sit back, hands behind my head, eyes sweeping the ceiling.

Yeah, Ramses might have stuck around for vengeance, but Eve's words—probably my subconscious, let's face it—linger with me. *"I was thinking about the coffee shop bombing, and I was wondering how Ramses or Gustavo might know how to build a bomb. What if they had an accomplice?"*

It's an interesting thought—one I'll talk to Eve about in the morning.

I like where the muse is taking me. The idea of rewriting the world, starting over—it feels like my story has a new beginning, this time with an ending I can live with.

And Butcher and Gabby are headed out for a long-awaited dinner.

CHAPTER 19

My muse is a fickle lover. When she's on, she's heat and fire and lightning in a silo and she infuses my body with a sort of ethereal creative power that takes over, rules and defies time.

I'm cast into my story for hours. Lost. The words pouring forth in a creative rush, a frenzy of insight, inspiration, and prose. I feel like I'm in the center of the universe, the exact place I'm supposed to be.

When she is done with me, I'm wrung out and wasted, yet the taste of her leaves me longing for more. But she will not be cajoled, and I know when I'm spent.

The night has waxed into dawn, the finest string of rose gold creeping into my den. I am stiff, and when I rise, I groan.

I love being a writer, the triumph of finishing something that is at once raw and brilliant, almost more satisfying than the thumping gavel of justice. At least with a book, I can write the ending I want; an ending we all want.

This time.

My muse has given me her best. My imagination takes a quick jog and I let the thought settle. I just might have a bestseller on my hands.

When I get up and pad to the door of my office, I notice the voices are gone, but light pulses from the family room. I wander in and see the television has gone to sleep, just the screen saver scrolling up the latest news. Eve forgot to turn off the volume, however, and when I click off the power, the buzz of the late night station vanishes.

I'm tired, but my body hums with the still too vivid memories so maybe I just need a hot shower.

And Eve. But I don't want to wake her at 5 a.m. Too early. There'll be time to tell her everything later.

The den used to be a guest room, and the bathroom off the entry is equipped with a shower. I heat it up, get in and stand under the spray, my arms braced against the wall.

Images assault me. Burke, young and with hair, that stupid soul patch.

Asher, and his Guns N' Roses T-shirt, *it's your funeral.* Clearly my imagination is conjuring him up to play a role in my subconscious.

There's Danny Mulligan and his warning. Maybe a remnant sliver of guilt. I did, technically, get her into trouble.

My mother's voice, fresh and bright and unslurred on the phone.

Happy Birthday, Dad.

Finally, John Booker. Alive, believing in me.

All pieces of my past, shattered, remade. My subconscious crafting a happy ending.

I soap up, rinse off and when I close my eyes, Ramses is there, his knife slicing into my kidneys.

My hand finds its way to where the wound was in the dream, as if it might be real.

I touch a rumple of flesh, and jerk.

What?

No. Not possible.

I twist my body to see it, but it's behind me, just above my hip. My hand seeks it again, and yes, *something* is there. A ridge of flesh, puckered up, but smooth.

Turning off the water, I step out into the humid, steamy air. Take a towel, wipe the sodden mirror and turn around, looking over my shoulder.

I just stare, my brain looping round and round, trying to make sense out of the scar. It's three inches wide, running at an angle from my hip into my back, thick and jagged and old. Nearly faded, reddened only by the spray of the shower.

Definitely a wound that could have been made by Ramses' dagger thrust just above my kidney.

My pulse has found my throat.

I grab a towel and wrap it around my waist and take the stairs fast. Ashley's door is closed, and I head straight for my bedroom.

I know Eve is asleep, but how can I not have a memory of being stabbed?

The bed is dark, just a form huddled along her side, Eve, as usual, wrapped up like a burrito. I tiptoe in and sit down on the edge. Put a hand on her shoulder. "Honey? Wake up."

My hand sinks into the body-sized wad and it takes only a second to realize that these are pillows, mounded up, as if pushed into a row.

I flick on the light.

On my side of the bed, the pillow is sunken, the sheets a wreck. As if I've torn them out, tossing and turning.

I've shoved the pillows to Eve's side of the bed.

"Eve?"

No answer.

The bathroom door is shut. I look for the thin strip of light that should be showing at the bottom of the door. Dark.

Where is she?

I grab a pair of jeans and get partially dressed, foregoing a shirt, and barrel downstairs, expecting to see her in the kitchen, maybe huddled up with a cup of coffee. She does that when she's brooding over a case, and I remember last night how she left the house for a run, restless and perturbed over a missing teenager.

But the kitchen is empty.

I stand at the window, staring out at the backyard.

It takes me a bit, but what I'm seeing—or *not* seeing—is dawning on me.

The swing set I spent last weekend building for Ashley is gone. Vanished.

Just grass, wild and unkempt, needing a mow.

Huh?

Behind me, a clock chimes. 6 a.m.

Eve has to be out for a run. I think this even as my brain shouts outs an unintelligible answer. Like my dream, I look around for it, as if the answer might materialize.

The doorbell rings, and my heart restarts.

It's Eve, and she's forgotten her keys.

I open the door and a rush of relief swills through me at the sight of Eve standing on the stoop. Except she's not wearing her running gear but a pair of dress pants, a crisp white shirt and she's carrying her satchel over her shoulder. Her beautiful hair is pulled back, tight, and her eyes hold age, stress, and not a little weariness.

The image of the younger Eve flashes through my mind. Bright, her hair down and flowing through my fingers. "Did you go back to work?" I ask and shift to my right to let her come inside. "Why didn't you text me?"

A car door slams and beyond her Silas is coming up the walk.

He has a scowl on his face, but I've secretly always thought that Silas wanted to kill me and bury me in a dumpster. What's strange, however, is that usually he hides it.

"Are you working from home today?" She isn't coming in.

"Stop it, Rem," she says, and her tone could peel skin.

Huh? I make the sound and she sighs.

"You can't keep dodging me. Grow up. I shouldn't have to ambush you to get you to accept these." While she's talking, she's dug out a manila envelope. She hands it to me. "Take them."

I admit that because of the way she says this, I'm slow to reach out and take the envelope. But I do, because she's Eve and I'll do just about anything she asks. I look at her and she glances away.

Her eyes glisten.

Silas stands behind her, glares at me, and I have the strangest sense he's here to protect her.

Ignoring the urge to put a hand to his chest, push hard and drag Eve off the stoop and into the house for a private chat, I open the envelope. My breath leaks out as I read the header.

"*Divorce* papers? What the hell, Eve?"

She wipes her hand across her cheek. "It's time, Rem, and you know it. I'm tired of waiting for you to get better, to snap out of it. We're both hurting, but you—I can't watch you destroy yourself."

Her words are like fists, each one slamming into me. "What are you talking about?"

"This." Her jaw tightens as she waves her hand at me. "The fact you won't admit you have a problem." She shakes her head. "I can smell the whiskey on your breath, Rem."

"That was hours ago." I'm not sure why, but I'm so desperate to find the Eve I know inside all that anger that I say, "I think I finished my novel. And it's good—really good."

She wears a strange expression, then her face crumbles and she presses her hand to her mouth, turning away.

"What?"

Silas moves a few inches closer to Eve. "Do you work at being the jerk of the century, Rembrandt? Or does is just come naturally? Please. Stop dreaming and start living in the world you created."

He puts a protective arm around Eve, *my* Eve.

I stand there, feet nailed to the cold entry way floor, bare chested and wet, the world spinning off its axis.

Especially when Eve looks up at me. "Just sign the papers, Rem, and let me go. Let Ashley go. It's over."

Ashley. The name rushes through me like wildfire. "Let her go? What are you talking about?"

I'm about ready to turn and sprint up the stairs to Ashley's bedroom when Eve gives me such a horrid, broken look I freeze. She draws in a breath and for a second, looks like she might slap me, venom in her eyes.

"I really hate you, Rembrandt Stone."

My jaw tightens, my throat raw. "Hate me all you want, but you're not taking my daughter away from me—"

"You're sick."

"Where is she, Eve?" My voice is louder than I want it to be, but fear is sneaking up from my gut and I can't help it.

"She's dead, Rem. She's *dead*, and you can't bring her back. So wake *up*!"

Her words sear through me.

No. *No*— "What are you *talking* about?"

She shakes her head, turns away.

"Rembrandt," Silas says, and his voice is oddly soft, as if I might be a hostage taker and he the friendly negotiator. "Ashley's murder was two years ago now. It's time to let go. I'm sorry."

My mouth opens, but nothing emerges. The urge to hurt him is gone, leaving me with nothing at all.

"Sign the papers," Eve says softly, tears cutting down her face. Behind her grief, I see the Eve I know, the Eve who has gone missing, the Eve I left behind last night. Strong, beautiful Eve who loves me, believes in me. Who sees exactly what this impossible news has done to me.

I stand there, mute, as Silas turns her, his arm curling around her shoulders, and walks her down our front steps. Helps her into the car. Drives her away from our home. Our family. Our life.

Taking the answers with her.

I back away from the door, glance at the envelope, then drop it onto the floor.

I take the stairs two at time.

I stop at Ashley's door, my hand on the knob, and close my eyes. Please, *no*.

My breath shudders as I swing the door in.

The shade is pulled, but the morning light cascades into an empty room. No wrapping paper from yesterday's gifts. No ponies cast about on the floor. Her stuffed animals are piled up on her bed, as if wondering, too, what happened.

My gaze falls on a teddy bear. Black, with a white star on its chest, the fur not yet rubbed off, the eye still intact.

Gomer.

My knees buckle and I crawl to the bed, yank it from the pile. Press it to my face.

No. No…*no…*

I'm shaking now, the world coming at me in splinters.

The wound.

The missing swing set.

My empty bed.

Eve on the porch with Silas.

And, on my daughter's shelf, a picture of my mother and father, grinning in a cruise line photo frame. They look happy, not a hint of my mother's stroke in her eyes, her smile.

She's dead, and you can't bring her back.

No.

I close my eyes and cling to the only fragment of all of this that makes any sense.

The only thing that offers the slimmest filament of hope.

Oh, God, *please.*

Let the watch work.

The epic series continues with Rembrandt Stone in two months.
Turn the page to check out a sneak peek of book two. Join us in
April for the next installment.

THE TRUE LIES
OF REMBRANDT STONE

NO UNTURNED STONE

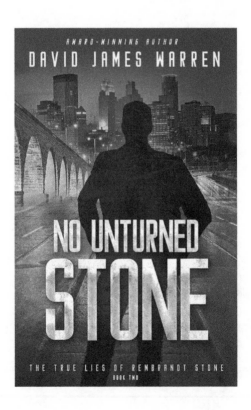

CHAPTER 1 - SNEAK PEAK

Just try and outrun your demons, I dare you.

I sit in my daughter's upstairs bedroom, in my half-remodeled craftsman, the morning bright against the window, holding a black teddy bear in my shaking hands. Gomer, a throwaway gift to my then four-year-old daughter, almost an afterthought I picked up from a drugstore as I raced home from work on a long-ago birthday.

A white star is embedded in the toy's fur, and this version of Gomer still has both eyes. They stare at me, black, glassy.

Shocked.

It's all wrong.

Please, God, let me wake up.

It's a fear that stalks every man, at least the ones like me, middle aged, married, a father of one, trying to frame his life into something that resembles success. A fear that, despite his heroic attempts, and as much as he tries to live in the light, his mistakes will find him.

And the price of those mistakes will cost him everything.

The voice that confirms it is seven years old, a deafening memory deep inside my head. "But daddy, you're a detective. You know how to find things."

Overnight my life has imploded.

My house is now a war zone, the product of fury and panic, the drawers opened, dumped out, my office bearing the wreckage of my disbelief. I spent the past hour digging through my belongings—our belongings—to find anything that might give me answers.

My seven-year-old daughter, Ashley, has vanished. No, that's not accurate. She's been murdered. Two years ago.

My beautiful wife, Eve, has left me. She wants a divorce from the man I've become.

A man I don't know.

And I haven't a clue how to get them back.

But I've jumped too far ahead. Ironically, I'll have to rewind time, return to the moment when the demons knocked on my door in the form of my ex-partner, a box of cold cases and a gift—an old watch bequeathed by my boss, Chief of Police, John Booker.

No, maybe I'll start later that night, when, after shaking awake from a nightmare, I stumbled downstairs to my office, the one with the less-than-inspirational leather chair my wife gave me when I left the force three years ago, and began to work on my unfinished novel.

Eve found me in the middle of the night as I sat there, barely dressed, trying to find words to add to my unfinished manuscript. She dragged out the cold cases and pulled the first one, the coffee-shop bombings of 1997, the one where we first met.

The catalyst for this entire nightmare.

That's when I put on the watch.

I couldn't believe Booker left me his prized possession. I don't remember a day he didn't wear it. An old watch with a worn leather wristband and a face like a vintage clock, the gears visible through the glass.

The hands didn't move, stuck on the five and the three, even when I wound it. On the back two words etched into the steel: Be Stalwart.

I hope so because this morning, when I realized what the watch had cost me, I threw it against the wall, snatched it off the floor and threw it again when it refused to work.

And you might think, calm down, Rembrandt, just get another watch.

But it's this watch that has somehow loosed the demons.

And I must find a way to send them back.

Now, as I sit in the wreckage of my life, I wiggle the dial again, shaking the watch, pressing it to my head. Please, please—

I don't really know what I'm asking for, because the truth is, well, unbelievable.

I dreamed—or did?—travel back in time. Solved the coffee shop bombing case. Woke up and everything...everything...

Oh, God—

"Rem?" A knock sounds on my open door—I didn't close it after Eve left, just an hour ago after handing me divorce papers. I remember dropping the packet on my rush up the stairs to Ashley's room to confirm Eve's wretched words.

"Ashley was murdered, remember? Two years ago."

I don't remember much after that.

"Rembrandt?" The voice makes me look up and probably it's a good thing the law just walked into the room because this is a crime scene.

My life has been stolen.

"Burke," I say, and I'm not even a little embarrassed that I've been crying. That my house looks vandalized. That I want to shake him for answers.

Andrew Burke was my partner for the better part of twenty years. A tall, bald, dark-skinned detective of the Minneapolis Police department, he's my best friend and sparring partner, even now.

Answers. He'll help me find them—

"Don't tell me you're on a bender again."

What?

Burke is wearing a suit, of course. I ditched mine after a few years on the job, but he always looked good in them. I was more of a sweater and jeans guy, and back then, I wore my hair long, with a hint of a beard, Don Johnson style. It was a thing. And Eve liked it.

Eve. The scene flashes through my mind again—Eve on the doorstep with her assistant, Silas. Eve handing me a manila envelope, Silas's arm around her. My insane urge to sink my fist into his mouth. Then the words—oh, God, the words—She's dead, Rem. She's dead, and you can't bring her back.

"No, I—" I stare again at Gomer, still in my grip.

"Aw, shoot," Burke says, his tone softening. "Eve told me you weren't doing well."

"Eve told you…"

"You fought again didn't you?"

My mouth opens and his words find the air around me, but don't land. Eve and I don't fight. At least, not about anything important. Sure, the occasional missed pickup at school, and she hates when I leave my socks on the stairs, but—

"I told her to wait and give you the divorce papers at work. I know yesterday was a hard day for you." He sighs, and I look back up at him. "I'm sorry man, but you knew this was coming."

I knew…

I can't breathe, my chest actually constricting, and I press my hand to it. Because twenty-four hours ago my wife was in my warm bed, my daughter in the next room surrounded by freshly unwrapped birthday gifts and my biggest trial was suffering from writer's block.

Then I had a dream—

No, then I…

I put my head between my knees.

"Rem! Sheesh, breathe." Burke leans down in front of me, his hand on my shoulder. "C'mon, don't do this to me again."

Again? But at least Burke is still my best friend, still the guy who won't let me drown.

"Dude. Listen, I get it. You're not the only one who wanted to forget yesterday's anniversary. But, it's been two years. Two." He draws a long breath. "It's time to at least try to move on."

I stare at him. "Ashley's dead." I am just trying out the words because, you know, she's not dead, not in my, um, timeline, my real timeline, but here— maybe here is all I have—

Now I can't breathe again.

"Yes," Burke says. "Yes she is." He sighs, and concern fills his dark eyes.

"How, when?" Because maybe if I have answers—

"No, Rem. We're not doing this again. You've read the file a thousand times."

The file. The file. In the box of files Booker gave me, all cold cases from my time on the job.

Maybe it's still here, sitting on the floor by the chair where Eve left it last night.

I toss Gomer aside, scramble past him, down the stairs and into my office.

I kneel beside the box, stacked high with folders, and rifle through them.

Stop, a coldness surging through me.It's gone. The file from the bombing case, the one I went back to solve—and yes, that still sounds crazy to me—

It's gone.

But of course it is. Because I, you know, solved it.

So it's not there. It can't be. But …

"What are you doing?" Burke says as he comes in and crouches again beside me.

"I'm just looking—" I see the cases I know too well. The working girl found near one of my favorite bars. A nurse, found in a parking lot in the middle of January. A waitress outside an uptown diner, and the worst—yes, it's still here.

I pull it out and groan.

The death of Eve's father, Minneapolis Deputy Police Inspector Danny Mulligan, and her kid brother, Asher. Skinny kid, smart, a hacker.

Asher saw me kiss Eve, and for a second the taste of her is on my lips. I kissed her last night, in her house, the smell of sawdust and summer in the air.

Real. The dream felt, smelled, and tasted real.

"It's not here." I set down Danny and Asher's file and keep looking, just to confirm.

"What's not there?"

"Ashley—where's her file?"

Burke is looking at me and now he shakes his head. "Get your head on and get down to the precinct. The Jackson murders aren't going to solve themselves." He turns away, runs his hand over his smooth head.

Last time I saw him, he had hair. That thought slides into my brain, and yes, maybe I'm having a nervous breakdown, a split with reality. He looks at me. "I know you're hurting, Rem, but you're freakin' me out."

Yeah, well, I'm freaking myself out too. But, "Where is Ashley's file?"

"C'mon, Rem."

"Tell me!"

"It's where it's been for the last two years! With all the other Jackson murders."

Who's Jackson? But I don't ask, because Burke is wearing a thin look. "Listen, I can't afford to have the head of the task force laying on his bathroom floor, drunk."

Again, drunk? Although, my gaze goes to my empty glass on the desk. One lousy shot of Macallans and suddenly I'm drunk?

Burke looks a little desperate now and it's an uncommon expression that unnerves me, too. "We finally caught a break—a survivor—and we need you on your game for this afternoon's press conference. We're close, Rem, you told me that yourself."

I did? But I nod. What I really want to do is bang my head on something, dislodge the memories that are stuck deep inside of a world I don't know, don't understand, but have clearly lived in.

He heads for the door. Pauses. "Come in, get to work. Please don't make me fire you."

Fire me? Burke is my boss?

I guess that feels right—I always knew he had leadership in him.

He leaves me there, and in a moment I hear his car drive away.

Work? Oh, I'm going to work all right.

To a job I remember quitting three years ago.

So the demons couldn't find me.

But apparently, I'll have to face those demons, if I want answers.

MEET
DAVID JAMES WARREN

Susan May Warren is the USA Today bestselling, Christy and RITA award–winning author of more than eighty novels whose compelling plots and unforgettable characters have won acclaim with readers and reviewers alike. The mother of four grown children, and married to her real-life hero for over 30 years, she loves travelling and telling stories about life, adventure and faith.

For exciting updates on her new releases, previous books, and more, visit her website at www.susanmaywarren.com.

James L. Rubart is 28 years old, but lives trapped inside an older man's body. He's the best-selling, Christy Hall of Fame author of ten novels and loves to send readers on mind-bending journeys they'll remember months after they finish one of his stories. He's dad to the two most outstanding sons on the planet and lives with his amazing wife on a small lake in eastern Washington.

More at http://jameslrubart.com/

David Curtis Warren is making his literary debut in these novels, and he's never been more excited. He looks forward to creating more riveting stories with Susie and Jim, as well as on his own. He's grateful for his co-writers, family, and faith, buoying him during the pandemic of 2020-21, and this writing and publishing process.

CPSIA information can be obtained
at www.ICGtesting.com
Printed in the USA
LVHW092205300721
694164LV00004B/183